D1708613

Books by Richard Jessup

THE CINCINNATI KID
THE RECREATION HALL

THE RECREATION HALL

THE RECREATION HALL

a novel by

RICHARD JESSUP

LITTLE, BROWN AND COMPANY
BOSTON — TORONTO

COPYRIGHT © 1967 BY RICHARD JESSUP

ALL RIGHTS RESERVED. NO PART OF THIS BOOK MAY BE REPRO-
DUCED IN ANY FORM OR BY ANY ELECTRONIC OR MECHANICAL
MEANS INCLUDING INFORMATION STORAGE AND RETRIEVAL
SYSTEMS WITHOUT PERMISSION IN WRITING FROM THE PUB-
LISHER, EXCEPT BY A REVIEWER WHO MAY QUOTE BRIEF PAS-
SAGES IN A REVIEW.

LIBRARY OF CONGRESS CATALOG CARD NO. 67–23833

FIRST EDITION

PZ
4
.J58
.Re

Emily Dickinson's poems "Not What We Did" and "Love Reckons
by Itself" are reprinted from *The Complete Poems of Emily
Dickinson* edited by Thomas H. Johnson, by permission of Little,
Brown and Company. Copyright 1929, © 1957 by Mary L.
Hampson. Copyright 1914, 1942 by Martha Dickinson Bianchi.

*Published simultaneously in Canada
by Little, Brown & Company (Canada) Limited*

PRINTED IN THE UNITED STATES OF AMERICA

For Arthur and Alan

with much appreciation

THE RECREATION HALL

1

It was a bright sunny day. As days go it left nothing to be desired. It was a day to start a war, or end one, or get drunk, or read the paper, or sail a ship, or make love to a beautiful woman, or any woman provided there was chemistry. But it would be a bad day if you did not care about anything at all. This good day, he saw, depended on what he made of it. This fine bright sunny day, like all other fine days, would be made up of internal decisions, big ones and little ones, and he had made a big decision and was over the line. That day and all other days to follow would be whatever he decided they would be. And when he discovered that it was entirely within himself, he did not feel so bad any more. He did not have to pass on the guilt, did not have to tar everybody with the same brush, or go hang John for his sins. He was Harry Cornell and truly nothing else mattered.

3

That morning he was putting the finishing touches on his dressing, and standing before the bedroom window absently adjusting his belt he looked down and saw a Cadillac convertible roll down the street. The Cadillac made Cornell think of Colonel Sami. There had been a few times in the past when Sami's kinfolk, dark swarthy men and distant lacquered women, would come to visit him, driving over from Baltimore or Washington, and twice from New York, and they all drove big black Cadillacs. When these visits took place Cornell would not see Colonel Sami at his usual table in The Recreation Hall for several days.

Below him the car braked sharply, and then he saw a column of children marching off to Sunday school; a few of the children registered surprise at the appearance of a Cadillac in St. Johns Landing, but this was quickly subdued by Miss Carrie, who herded them along. Cornell's son, a six-year-old blond boy who looked like his mother, joined the end of the line. When the children had passed safely across the street the Cadillac lazed through the intersection. He could not see the face of the driver, a woman, alone, and he put her down as a tourist and not one of Sami's friends. Behind him a door opened and closed but he did not turn around. He finished his dressing and stared into the summer distance which that morning was misty with humidity and promised a scorcher. It reminded him of going to Lake Pontchartrain in New Orleans when he was a boy. Singing birds, laughing children and stuttering lawn mowers were all of a part and seemed to be reminding him that he had, somehow, come to this. He smiled. So this is disenchantment.

— I had hoped, his wife said, that we would never have to go through another night like we did last night.

She had not moved from the door and stood leaning against it. She was still in her robe and gown, a thin small-breasted woman with yellow hair caught at the nape with a blue ribbon. Her face was drawn. He did not reply until the church bell, tolling sadly in worn frag-mented notes, was quiet. The summer noises drifted back up to him out of the silence. He glanced at his wife briefly. They were the same age only she looked much younger.

— Sorry.

— Is that all you've got to say?

— If you'd sleep with me willingly, Delila, we wouldn't have to—

— I told you I had a headache, she said, cutting him off.

— You've had a headache every time I've touched you for the last six years—since the boy was born.

— Not *every* time! she said. You bruised my thighs and you nearly tore off my breast. She ran her hand up and felt her tender bosom.

Shifting his resentment, closing out his anger and his sudden hate, shaking his head as if it would dismiss her hate, he answered coldly. He glanced at her again, briefly.

5

— Sorry.

— It was rape.

He did not reply.

— And it *is* rape every time you touch me.

— Goddammit, Delila, you can't have it both ways.

— What is that supposed to mean? Something disgusting from your bachelor days, I guess.

Startled, seeing and understanding instantly her twisting of his innocent remark, it helped for the moment to ease off his anger. He ignored the question and walked to the dresser, taking his watch and strapping it on. Looking at her again briefly, noting her thin lips and nervous hands pulling at the bodice of her robe, he was drawn back to the question and considered it. In the seven years they had been married there had been three times, just three, that quite unexpectedly he had rolled over in the middle of the night to take her, waking her out of a deep sleep and tearing into her hard and fast before she knew what was happening, and on all three occasions she had, and he had thought about this, been ravenous, whispering in his ear, urging him on.

— Now—now—again—now harder—!

But he had never let her know this. It was not his way to use this ammunition against her when they got into one of their fights. He stuffed a clean handkerchief into his pocket, speaking to her easily, not allowing recrimination to creep into his voice.

— Nothing disgusting, Delila, it was just a figure of speech, and— He paused, shrugged, not continuing and

6

gazed out of the window. He had a clear view of the river from this window and he studied the deep dark hills on the other side. The hills were darker because of the humidity and he reminded himself to have Terrible turn the air conditioning on as soon as he opened The Hall.

— Well?

— Well, what? he asked in a finely controlled voice.

— Finish what you were saying.

— I've forgotten.

— You have not!

— I have, and—well, forget it, Delila. It looks like a nice day.

— Goddamn the nice day and I will *not* forget it. Finish what you were saying.

— But you've heard it so many times, he said patiently. And it never seems to penetrate.

— Tell me.

— All right. I'll protect your sensibilities, and your reputation—

— What about my reputation?

— as a loving wife and mother—

— You *discuss* me and our affairs in that revolting place? I knew it. I *knew* it!

— The Recreation Hall pays the rent and keeps us both eating and makes us both respectable. And I don't discuss you, or our affairs, or anything personal with anyone, anywhere. He stopped, shrugging again, not knowing, not caring what he wanted to say, turning to listen to the choral voices of the children in Sunday school yelling out their arrogant, however innocent, confidence.

Jesus loves me, this I know—!

— Your reputation here in St. Johns Landing, he said, studying again the dark early summer hills across the river, and refrain—
— Refrain from what?
He spoke dreamily, innocently, wondering about the love of Jesus for the pellagra children of a dozen countries he had been to or for the children the Germans had thrown into the ovens.

For a Bible tells me so!

— Finish what you were saying.
— Oh, he said still dreamily, refrain from going over to Baltimore and enjoying some of that fresh young pussy they ship—
— What!
— up from the farms around Tidewater and the Eastern Shore. I'll protect your reputation—but you've got to behave.
— *What did you say!*
He was angry again, not with her but with himself, and because he really understood his wife, he was ashamed. A very long time ago he had realized and

8

understood that his wife was not bright or clever or witty—was in fact ordinary. Travel around the world and his years at sea had taught him how easily the unsophisticated and the untalented could be hurt and he had seen enough of it in his lifetime to have a strong reaction to thoughtless cruelty. She seized on the remark and her tears, large and copious, flowed down her cheeks and she swept across the room.

— Whores, she said, her voice quivering in an accusing whisper. I might have known.

— No, he said. No, you're wrong and you've twisted things again. No whores. I've never touched another woman since we've been married. It's just a fact that they're there—in Baltimore—waiting—and I have this problem—and—

— *Don't you ever force me again!*

He fought back against the building pressures and feeling himself losing against them, knowing that it was not only this fight but the overwhelming history of their marriage of many such times and he did not want to let go.

— I've given you an alternative, don't you see that? he said and he felt his voice edging toward cold command, the quarterdeck voice he called it, when there was no questioning his authority. And I'll take you Delila, anytime I want you, anywhere I want you, and don't think otherwise.

— There isn't a fiber of love for me in your body. I'm

9

something to throw on the bed and violate—to give it to—for your pleasure.

— Believe me, Delila, with you it is not pleasure.

She stopped crying and stared at him. Thoughtless cruelty again, and he was, he knew, reacting to the building pressure. He had to get out of there. He tried once more to shake it off and turned to the window to search the invitational hills, keeping what secrets in their summer foliage he could not imagine, but waiting for him to come and explore them, beckoning to him through the haze of the rising humidity. He saw the Cadillac again, and again he could not see the woman's face. He searched the details: back seat piled high with expensive-looking luggage and a fur coat on the front seat beside her. Her manner was deliberate and there was something more than just out of place with her being in St. Johns Landing. An aura of the big city? he thought, and then she was gone from view. He was surprised to find himself talking when he came out of his speculation about the woman in the Cadillac.

— *and* whatever you've got in that narrow mind of yours, Delila, you'd better forget it. We've floated into a pattern of behavior, and for some reason that I cannot fully understand, it must fit, and we act out this charade every Sunday morning or sometimes Saturday nights, and you threaten and get hysterical and I feel like a goddamn stud bull—

— Don't you ever—*ever* come at me again.

— You see, you don't even try to understand when I talk to you.

— Did you hear what I said? Don't you ever come at me again and force me *again!*

— Or you'll what?

— I'll do something terrible to you, Harry, I swear to God I will. Something that will take care of that lust of yours for the rest of your life.

— No, you won't, he said calmly.

— Won't I. I *will!*

He picked up his keys from the dresser and stooped to open the bottom drawer. He took out a small hand safe made of good steel, and twirling the combination, opened it and took out several bills. He then wrote in a small accounting book:

Sunday, May 1st $50.00 Shf. Cabell

He returned the book to the safe, closed it and closed the drawer. Delila was standing by the bed not looking at him, her hands nervously fluttering at her robe again.

— Whores, she said. I might have known.

He passed to the door, glanced at her again, briefly, and went out.

— Whores! she screamed at him.

He stepped back into the room and they stared at each other and finally he spoke.

— Go on to church, Delila, he said.

— *Whores!* she screamed in his face. And you made me one too!

— I'm sorry about your thighs and your breast. I really am.

11

Cornell saw the woman in the Cadillac again the moment he stepped from the house. She passed by and stared at him. He saw a beautiful woman with a pale face and exquisite nose and a full but rigid mouth: it was the kind of mouth that had been set against many hard decisions. She wore large sunglasses and he could not see her eyes, but it was the set of the mouth that attracted his attention. He turned his back on her and then glanced up and saw his wife watching him from the window. He walked away and at the corner turned down a small lane that smelled of loop vine and May rose.

2

He was a tall man with probing dark eyes and at thirty-eight had recently discovered that a life he knew perfectly and that he had been living a very certain way for as long as he had been in St. Johns Landing was beginning to fail him. He considered the failure a penalty but he did not let it throw him, and making a slight adjustment he went on, letting the idea of there being nothing else for him to win or lose take its place alongside other penalties he had learned to live with since marrying Delila seven years before and quitting the sea. He was a quiet man and did not talk about himself and no one knew he was living with this thing which he described to himself as a loss of magic.

Harry Cornell did not want to talk to anyone, nor even see anyone. Encouraged by the viciousness of his fight with Delila, his natural choice of being a loner and possessing a genuine contempt for those who indulged in useless conversation, he knew his trip that morning to Cabell's was going to be difficult. In a lifetime he had learned to recognize the mood he was in at the moment, and felt the pressures going over the top. He had many tricks to evade the grinding anger, but none of them were working for him that morning.

He walked into Cabell's Lane, turning into the shade. He could hear the convulsive cough of the Sheriff a half-block away. He walked steadily, hoping his mood and his hate would ease, yet being unwilling to slow his pace or take a turn around the block. If Cabell was in his way, then Cabell would have to move aside. That was the way it was. It was that simple.

He wiped whiskey sweat from his face. He had drunk too much the night before. He always drank on Saturday nights anticipating his ritual rape of Delila, but last night he had gone too far. He did not feel guilty about being rough with his wife. It was simply an error in judgment: he had taken several too many drinks and instead of going home with a warm buzz, letting the alcohol dissipate Delila's cold resistance as he sweet-talked and eased her into seduction, he had been cold and brutal about it. Without any preparation he had forced her legs apart and holding her in an iron grip had ravaged her.

He slowed his pace and came to a stop and stood under an oak tree. He wiped sweat from his eyes. He sighed and closed his eyes. He was aware that he was working on an internal decision and that he was reject-

14

ing his environment, denying his place, and that he was doing it deliberately. Yet he knew that if he continued as he was, he would rot. The decay was already apparent. He was alone and there was nothing he could do about it.

At what point had life turned sour on him? Where had he lost it? Where it was once good, it was now bad. Where had it gone wrong for him? Not only was his true selfishness missing, but he saw clearly that gone too was that furious indifference to ambition, hope for the future, arrogance in the face of uncertainty, always moving ahead into the new time, a picture-book man of insolence, of which he had been so proud. All gone. Had it started as far back as his last few trips to sea, before meeting and marrying Delila? Or had it started with Delila? He was reluctant to accuse Delila. He understood how elusive reason and logic became when the pounding hardness of a prick and the hot musk of a woman on a summer night was the combination. For whatever reason it was surely gone. As the darkness is gone from the North Atlantic storm after you have battled your fears and the storm all night, as the short time with a whore is gone after you've sweated her out for the last two weeks of a crossing, as a full bottle of whiskey is gone when it is the only one you have.

Harry Cornell knew all about reality. He had lived, since escaping at the age of fifteen from a brutalizing father, in a harsh pragmatic world of compromise. He had no use at all for the suckers who strove for the ideal. He had never known a true winner in his whole life, and always, if he dug deeply enough below the surface he would *find* the compromise, the fix, the sentimentality and the rationalizing candor of muscle. For him reality was something that always had the edge and could always slap you down. But there was a way to beat reality: you didn't lie, you didn't cheat, you didn't steal and you always held honor for yourself. Once these sentiments had been satisfied, then you could compromise your way straight to heaven or hell. There was only one rule. It did absolutely no good to be on your guard for the slap-downs. He had forecast early in his life that to be constantly on your guard only produced a hostility that asked for trouble.

— Well, now this, and what's to come, he said aloud and lunged out of the shade and walked easier down the lane, reasonably sure he no longer belonged. He was not even curious which way he would go or when it would happen. He wheeled into Cabell's rose garden and walked directly to the back door, knocked several times as a warning and then entered.

3

It was a quiet kitchen, built with thick walls to be cool in the summer, and it was. Cabell sat at the kitchen table and read a throwaway comic book that came with the Sunday paper. He looked over the top of his glasses.

Their gaze was direct and held long for a hard meaningful moment. They had their opinions of each other, and neither man was afraid to show them. A homey kitchen, filled with the quick-at-hand things needed every day. Coffee perked to one side. A .38 and harness was slung over the back of a chair. The .38 had an eight-inch-long barrel for accuracy. The Sheriff prided himself on his marksmanship.

— I bet I won on that horse, didn't I? the Sheriff said.

Cornell placed the fifty dollars on the table and backed away. He replied in a calm flat way.

— Won as usual, Sheriff.

— I never lose. Ain't it a shame the way I pick winners? The Sheriff put the money in his pocket.

Cornell took a cup and poured a taste of coffee in the bottom. The Sheriff continued with the comic book. The game of winning on the horses was over. The graft had been paid. Cornell stared out into the rose garden, which was the finest in St. Johns Landing. But the Sheriff did not like roses. It was his wife, a small and strictured woman fifteen years younger than her husband, who had developed the garden. Cornell loved to look at them but did not care for the perfume.

— How was the party last night? Cornell asked.

— Ummhh? The Sheriff, concentrating on the comic book, did not look up. He spoke again, an elaborate patronizing tone. What's that you say?

Cornell waited. He knew his man by now.

— You asked about the party? Tom Tyson, Miles Walker and Chigger are still partying. We half expected you, the Sheriff said.

— You had women, didn't you?

— Four of Miz Pitt's prettiest over from Winchester. Boy! Let me tell you—

— Some other time, Cornell said harshly. He stepped through the door into the garden without looking back. The Sheriff followed him.

— Got any reason for not having a party now and then?

— No reason, Cornell said.

— That don't make sense.

— You weren't asked to understand, Cabell. You just make up your mind and live with it.

— It's a moral position—

— No.

— and I always think a man's a little bit of a liar if he hides behind a moral position when it comes to women.

— So now I'm a liar, Cornell said, turning.

The Sheriff grinned. He scratched his armpit. He didn't reply and continued to grin and scratch.

— You're a fat-gutted sonofabitch, Sheriff. You don't like me and I don't like you. But that's okay, so long as you don't get too close to me. I pay your little graft—

— You called me a sonofabitch, boy, Cabell said, still grinning.

I'll take it back, Cornell said. You're a no-good, fat-gutted sonofabitch.

— Your dander is *up!* the Sheriff said breaking out into laughter.

Cornell walked out of the garden and into the lane. It could be thought that you are less innocent than you pretend you are. What is the difference between naked arrogance and arrogance with grace? There is no difference, he decided, since the result, the effect is the same. He had been arrogant with grace with Delila that morning and he had been nakedly arrogant with Cabell. Both were touched, both had been stung.

He felt no regret as he walked down the lane and it was because he felt nothing that he knew his internal decision had been a true decision. It was over. He was, from that moment on, forever committed to what came next and it did not include anything that had ever happened to him before, or that he had ever been concerned with before.

Perhaps he should leave now. Just walk away from it. All of it. The Recreation Hall, his pretense with Delila, his difficult love for his son, his place in St. Johns Landing. Why not?

The Cadillac rolled around the corner and the woman turned to look at him from behind the dark glasses. The big car eased on out of sight and Cornell continued his walk toward The Recreation Hall.

When he stepped out into the brilliant sunlight of Main Street he saw Terrible waiting for him across the street. A powerfully built Negro in a white mess jacket, Terrible's gray hair was thick and tufted, framing a perfect head and a face the color of iodine. At the same time, glancing the other way, he saw Colonel Sami move around the corner, a thin immaculate man with an erect military bearing. He wore a snow-white suit, shirt and tie and Panama hat. He carried a cane and limped slightly. European-style sunglasses, perfectly round with wire rims and frames, blocked out his eyes. The glasses were as big as silver dollars and he never took them off, indoors or out. Sami's face was heavily pitted from a bout with acne as a youth. Sharp-featured and intent, stylized and mannered, he walked down the sidewalk in the brilliant sunlight, pausing only slightly to watch the

Cadillac. Cornell had another, closer look at her this time as she passed, but she did not look at him, and he continued on toward The Recreation Hall. She was not, he decided, as young as she would pretend to be.

— Good morning Harry, Terrible, Colonel Sami said as the three men stood before the double doors of the building. He spoke with an English accent.

— Morning, Colonel, Terrible replied. Mistuh Cornell.

Cornell nodded and began opening the door. Neither of the three men thought about it and it was never planned, yet they managed five days out of the week to arrive at the door within a few steps of each other. Rarely was Cornell first. The door was opened and sunlight poured into the dark, quiet, inviting interior. Cornell moved inside, a quick inquisitive eye examining, not really curious or fearful that something might be wrong, but because it was something real and not imagined and that he had created and that he enjoyed and that belonged totally to him.

Colonel Sami, a Syrian, claimed to be the only non-Aryan to achieve the rank of colonel in the Nazi SS. Sami also claimed many triumphs against the French and British during the war. This may or may not have been true as far as the people of St. Johns Landing were concerned, and there was a wallet photograph of Sami and the Mufti standing before a Middle Eastern street scene. But there was no way to prove him a liar and St. Johns Landing could not have cared less; indeed, this would have been true even if they knew who the Mufti was, which they did not. Sami was emphatically, and to them accurately, the Greek who came over from Europe to claim old Ba-Yusef's house and apple orchards. Ba-Yusef, who had also been known as the Greek, had been respected and had established himself in St. Johns Landing over a period of sixty-five years, building two of the finest orchards in the area, side by side on the Winchester Road running for two miles. He had dealt fairly, if shrewdly, and the people of the countryside were genuinely sorry when Ba-Yusef died. They did not know and were not interested in getting to know Sami, Ba-Yusef's cousin. Sami was the New Greek, or Yusef's Kin, or among the truculent, the Greaser. Only Harry Cornell knew that Sami had been a true colonel in the SS and that he had turned traitor against his country and the Nazis when the OSS had contacted him and advised him of his inheritance, offering him a guarantee of immunity if he would become an agent for the Allies. Harry Cornell learned about it simply because he was the only one who saw and talked with Sami regularly.

Aside from the greeting at the door, nothing was said between the three men as they entered the huge, dark, quiet room, each going his own way. The Colonel moved to one of the wrought-iron tables, placed his hat and cane on the white marble top and sat down facing the open door. Cornell moved behind the bar, walking directly to a small locked drawer. He removed several worn cotton money bags, opened the cash register, and

emptied the change and the few bills into the compart-
ments. Terrible opened the back door leading to the
garden and then stepped to the huge refrigerator that
filled nearly half of the rear wall. He took out a bottle of
white wine, examined the label and sighted the contents
against the sun-filled front door. Cornell had finished
with his change-making when Terrible moved behind
the bar, and as the bottle was opened Cornell turned to a
twelve-foot-long shelf of record albums. He began to
flip them quickly, hesitating over one and then going on,
and with his free hand reaching over to turn on an
expensive stereo phonograph.

Terrible opened the wine, and with great care selected
a glass and walked to the Colonel's table, waiting patiently while the Colonel breathed, sipped and tasted. He
nodded and Terrible poured a glass and left the bottle
while he went off to prepare an ice bucket. The Colonel
lighted a cigarette, sipped the wine and waited. A
moment later the revelation of Mahler's Symphony No.
1 flooded the room. The Colonel smoked his cigarette
and sipped his wine and he stared out into the sun-filled
street. Cornell moved to the end of the bar nearest the
windows and stood, one foot raised to the shelf ledge,
and he too stared into Main Street. Terrible returned
with the ice bucket, placed the bottle deep inside and
wrapped the neck with a linen cloth; he turned on the
air-conditioning, picked up a brush and began to work
on the felt of the pool table, brushing it with an infinite
patience and timeless care. Another day had begun.

Without apparent notice of each other, moving in their own polarized and distinctive established pattern, they settled into the familiar and the comforting.

— Who is she? Sami asked.

— I don't know. Never saw her before, Cornell replied without turning.

— And you, Terrible?

— Ah don' know, Colonel, suh.

A bell, much like a doorbell, rang and Terrible moved immediately to the back door. Cornell and the Colonel paid no attention. At the door Terrible turned thoughtfully.

— Might be a lost tourist, uh, Mistuh Harry? Getting no reaction, Terrible moved through the door.

The Cadillac moved down Main Street and past their view again, a slight movement of the woman's head as she caught the music coming from the Hall was noticed by both of them, then she was gone again.

— Terrible is wrong. She is not a tourist. She is here with reason, Colonel Sami said.

— Think so?

— She has been driving all over town all morning. I have been watching her. She is looking as though she was remembering.

— You can see that, huh?

— It is my opinion, Sami said. And she reminds me of a woman.

— Tell me about her, Sami, Cornell said.

24

— Harry, have you never heard of Oktoberfest?

— No, tell me about that, and the woman too, Cornell said.

— An attack on the Russian Front. I helped Otto Shef himself prepare the maps. Oktoberfest is a German festival—it was a code name.

— Tell me about that too, Cornell said. He had not moved but continued to look out into the street, a dead expression on his face. Tell me about the woman, Oktoberfest and Otto Shef's mapmaking for the attack on the Russians. It was the request of a man with an intense vacuum to fill. He realized that it had been a vacuum for six years.

Colonel Sami sipped his wine and refilled the glass, lighted another cigarette, and eased the cramp in his bad leg.

— I saw Otto in New York last year when I went for a visit and to have my leg checked—do you remember, Harry?

— Yes, I remember. Tell me about that too, Sami.

— I reminded Otto of our greatest effort in the war. It was a professionally planned effort worthy of anyone. And Otto, he said to me, New York is crawling with ex-German officers. Ex's he called them. Then he said that he would remember me as the command officer of Oktoberfest, instead of just another old Nazi colonel who had managed to escape to America. The Colonel sipped his wine and patted his lips with his fingers. He chuckled appreciatively to himself. Actually I was not the command officer. But it was nice of Otto to say so, don't you think, Harry?

— Tell me about why you think he said that to you, Sami.

— Oh, obvious enough. He wanted to be invited here, to St. Johns Landing.

— But you weren't extending invitations, were you?

— He was always a snob. Typical middle-class Prussian.

Terrible entered from the back door and walked to the service bar and Cornell turned to look at him.

— It's Miz Josephine DuPays, Mistuh Harry. She want a double shot of rye and please, suh, put on the Brahms like you always do on Sunday morning. She don't like this one.

Cornell nodded and poured a good four ounces of whiskey into a glass as Terrible turned to get water and a bowl of ice. Terrible was careful in his selection of a cut-glass vase which he filled with water and then put several garden flowers into it. The Mahler was cut short and Cornell took a Brahms album down from the shelf without looking. Brahm's First Symphony now filled the room and Colonel Sami nodded in agreement. Cornell moved to a back window and looked out into the garden, filled with loop vine and May rose that curled through thick stands of bamboo. A high wall isolated the garden from buildings nearby, and tables and chairs like those inside the Hall were shaded and softened by umbrellas. Two all-weather stereo speakers were hidden in the bamboo.

Josephine DuPays sat straight backed and rigid as Terrible approached her with the tray. A woman of seventy, she wore a choker and was the Lady of Quality out of a Victorian parlor. Her hands, as she raised the drink, with Terrible standing at her elbow watching her apprehensively, shook only a little. She managed to get half the drink down and then put the glass on the table, firmly. She raised her eyes to Terrible's face. There was a flash of victory or triumph in her expression that she had not spilled a drop. Terrible smiled and nodded.

— This looks like it's going to be one of your good days, Miz DuPays.

Cornell turned away from the back window, moving behind the bar and returning to his vantage point at the front, and stood watching the street.

— How is she this morning?

— She got half of it down without help from Terrible.

— That is very nice, Sami said. Why does she drink? To shake off the ghost of old illusions, I suppose, illusions that robbed her of whatever life she might have had.

— She's been a drunk since she was sixteen, Cornell said.

— I don't believe that, Sami said.

— Go ask her.

— How could I ask such a question of a lady? If she

says yes, it only proves that you are not a liar, and she has been forced to face an indiscretion—if she says no, then I have been a cad by asking such a question. Still, I do not believe you, Harry.

Cornell moved away from the window and turned to the bar. He began a slow systematic examination of each bottle on the marble shelf. Not once did he look at himself in the deep honest mirror.

— Tell me about the woman, Sami.

— What woman?

— Tell me about Oktoberfest.

— Oh, that—

— And your trip to New York.

— Harry, you're mad today. I shall be quiet.

— No, I want you to talk. Tell me things. Truths, half-truths, lies, big ones and little ones. Tell me about illusion. That should be interesting.

— One cannot live without illusions.

— That's a good beginning, go on.

— And one cannot live with them.

— An old Nazi like you should know about illusions, I guess.

— Don't be nasty, Harry.

— Or is it delusions?

— Harry—

— How does it feel to be a living liar to the whole human race, Colonel?

— Why are you here, Harry—in this place, St. Johns Landing? You know, I have a theory about you—

— Save it, Cornell said savagely. He continued to examine the bottles, removing those nearly empty and setting them out to be replaced with full ones by Terrible.

— Unwilling to face certain truths, or lies, about yourself, Harry.

— Don't get personal, Colonel. You lost that right when you and the rest of the rats stoked the first of the ovens.

— Ahh! That one. Sami breathed deeply and they were both silent for the length of time it took Cornell to finish his examination of the bottles. He turned when the last bottle was removed. It was over. He glanced around as if looking for something else to do. His shoulders slumped and he walked back to his place at the front.

— One cannot live with illusions, my dear Harry, after a life of delusions. Consider what I say for a moment.

Cornell was silent, turning his head to watch the street.

— Whatever I am, and believe me, that isn't much, and whatever I become in the future, I know what I am now at this moment. I am a fifty-eight-year-old ex-German officer who was fortunate enough to have important friends in the State Department who secured for me my inheritance. I am grateful. You don't know how grateful a man can be, Harry, until you have your life handed back to you, regardless of the motives or the circumstances, and you are allowed to meet your own conscience and your own guilts on your own terms.

— You do, I suppose, living up there in old Ba-Yusef's brick mansion?

— It is not something that can be discussed. To talk about it would be to confuse my expiation.

— Do you cry, Sami?

— No.

— So you sleep?

— Yes.

— Don't you take a trip over to Mrs. Pitt's in Winchester now and then?

— Yes.

— Then where's the hangup? Where do you and in what form do you expiate?

— I do not allow myself the luxury of making any kind of decision, Harry. That is my purge, my conscience.

Cornell turned and looked at the blank, pockmarked face that was as expressionless as ever and as hidden, as secretive, behind the sunglasses. It was not the answer he expected.

— Colonel, I apologize. I'm in no position to accuse anybody of anything.

— That's the most conversation we've had in all these years, Harry.

— Is it? Cornell moved slightly for a better view of something in the street. Don't let it go to your head. They had in fact discussed, or nearly discussed, the

Colonel's conscience many times. But in the past Cornell had always cut it off before getting too involved. But his thoughts and guilts about the fight with Delila that morning had disturbed him.

— I've often speculated on why you tolerate me day after day—

— You pay your bar bill on time.

— Not a feeling, an understanding for the underdog, the loser?

Cornell moved directly to the door, speaking over his shoulder.

— I called you a rat, not a loser or an underdog. Yes, ma'am, can I help you? He blocked the door.

She stepped inside. Stunning in a middle-aged, mature female way that was all chic and cynicism, there was a smell about her, one of female musk and expensive perfume, as right as rain and irresistible. She stood perfectly still and stared coolly into Cornell's eyes. Then she turned away from Cornell's deadpan, blatant stare and examined the room.

— I don't know. A drink, maybe.

— Yes, ma'am, Cornell said, his voice flat. Step right over to the bar, or if you prefer, a table. Or if you'd further prefer, we have a ladies' garden out back.

— Further prefer? she asked and before Cornell could reply she stepped past him. The bar will do.

Cornell did not move, but spoke, turning slightly and observing her from the rear.

— The garden's rather nice. Right now, Miz Josephine

DuPays is out there—by herself—taking her morning shot. She's a little hung over, but she's a nice lady and she might like drinking company.

— An ice cold martini please. Very dry. Very cold.

4

Earlier that day she had swept the Cadillac convertible over the top of a fat, broad-backed hill and all of it lay before her just as she had remembered it, spread in layers of green, hill rising into hill, with wild messenger pigeons wheeling in the incredible summer sky; wanting to study it, she had pulled into a gas station.

It was still the fair country she had remembered all the time she had been away, and when she saw it again, a soft and lovely land, fair to the eye and soothing, she was sure she had made the right decision and that she would be able to take from this place that she knew so well and go on. It was not too late, she kept reassuring herself, and though she had made a hell of a mess of things until now, here in St. Johns Landing she would take a long rest and find a reason for going on.

The scene was immediately familiar to her. To her left in the direction of the Saddle, where it was said Lincoln's mother was born, sheep grazed; to her right was a road she knew from her childhood which led to Antietam battlefield, which claimed more American lives than any other battlefield in any other war, and beyond this road, spreading fanlike over the hills and orchards and fields was Harpers Ferry and, though she could not see it, the upper Potomac where the river made a slash cut like the scar of a fresh wound; her senses were assaulted by the sweet springtime scent of honeysuckle, May rose and loop vine.

She walked to the edge of the weed patch at the back of the cotton-gin building with the gas attendant, an old man with a thin body and a self-pitying smile etched into his face, watching her carefully. Flies buzzed and she washed them away with a gloved hand; a bird called, a single lucid note, and was answered by its mate with an equally clear and lucid note; the soft tinkle of the toll bell within the gas pump emphasized the quiet morning. She stood beside a tangle of brush and wild hedge and pulled off her gloves before crushing several leaves in her palm, lifting them to her face and breathing in the soft perfumed fragrance.

— That's loop vine, missus, the old man said to her, speaking from across the driveway. Around here there's a saying that if a maiden lady takes loop vine leaves to her bosom on the night of May first, she will dream of the man she'll marry before the frost comes.

She ignored the old man's comments: she knew about

the loop vine legend and the strange cycle that brought lavender perfume once every ten years. How much? she asked, a hard and direct, almost metallic sound that she had picked up long ago and that had cut her escorts effectively when they became too sportive.

She responded to seeing it all again as she rolled down the hill and into the first of the valley regions. She would see something she remembered and then try to press her memory into anticipating what would be next beyond that house or that barn or that old tree. She was nearly always right. And then she was there, at the turnoff of the main highway and into the small narrow road that would take her down a mile-long hill and straight into the Potomac River. Her heart beat a little faster and her emotions began to rise, but she kept them in check: just one more thing she had learned in New York in eighteen years. *Goddamn New York!* she thought.

When she heard the bells, she remembered it was Sunday. She saw men and women standing on their porches dressed in their Sunday best, or children moving about stiffly near the door waiting for the family. They stared at her and she stared back from behind the screen of her sunglasses; she had on her Chanel suit and a silk blouse, and with the car weighted and piled high with her luggage and in that sunlight and in that town and in that car she knew exactly what the people waiting to go to church thought of her when she rolled past them down, down, down toward the river.

It was an abstract street: it remained fixed in the

35

mind—etched there by its simplicity and because it was like entering bodily into a poem.

It was not a large town and the main street was not very long. From the town limits it was exactly nine blocks to the river bend and the Cadillac rolled down the middle of the street in a slow, almost funereal pace and she greeted each sad and melancholy memory as though she were accepting homage from lost loves. *Dorie!* a paternal voice cautioned a child on her left, a small delicate little girl who stared openly at her. Yes, she knew exactly what she looked like. New York again: conscious awareness of one's set and style. *Goddamn New York!*

It was a pre-Revolutionary town of white clapboard, red brick and tin roofs. Small, clean, swept, painted and genuine without any touristy tricks. Droggman's Stationery Store was still there with a stack of Sunday papers on the outside bench. Mr. Droggman had let her read all of the magazines so long as she did not mess them up and she pretended she did not know that Mr. Droggman brushed her a little too closely in the narrow space behind the counters. Harvey's Drygoods and Notions Store with the same Gibson Girl store dummy still in the window: everything she wore until she was fifteen had been purchased in Harvey's. Now she was at a hardware store with a window display of sheet-metal vents, shanty pipes and chicken feeders. Lastly the printing shop where one hundred sixty years ago the St. Johns *Press* had argued against the Louisiana Purchase, only now it was something called The Recreation Hall.

Except for the bells, the thoroughbred silence of the Cadillac and the springtime noises, there was no other sound and she did not see the children ahead of her. She slammed on her brakes and the huge car rocked as if in a cradle, then in military precision the boys and girls in their Sunday blacks and whites marched across the lane before the car. She took time to light a cigarette and to stare from behind the security of her sunglasses at St. Johns Landing resplendent in a Sunday morning pastime.

She drove back and forth in town, taking side streets, rolling up and down rose-covered lanes, tree-shaded channels, and all the while breathing in the lavender of the ten-year loop vine. Twice again she had to brake sharply as the same group of Sunday school children marched like driver ants across the streets before her.

When she had toured all of it she turned toward the river. The Old Bridge had been destroyed and its high Romanesque arches of granite ledge had, over three-quarters of a century, collected fill and dust and bird droppings from the air, and each column, standing like a sentinel in the middle of the quiet pool, was covered with a crown of greenery, intense and spectacular in spring essence. It reminded her of a Piranesi etching of a wasted Rome. She parked the car and walked to the edge of the Old Bridge where there were still in place the foundation approaches. Above the green and now, because of the mid morning sunlight, golden river she studied her reflection: it was time, she thought, speaking silently to her reflection, to get on with new business. It

37

was going to be difficult to forget the life of good hunger she had lived, but it was over, and having seen what happened to others who stayed too long after the party was over, she knew it was time to get out. On a recent trip to Boston to cover the opening of a new play, a city she ordinarily felt close and intimate with, she had become so desperate for identity she had gone alone to a bar where she knew they would say hello to her. And when she realized what she had done, she began asking questions about her life and getting no answers that added up, she knew it was over. But there was more evidence than just a single hopeless night in Boston where a half-drunken woman fashion editor might have felt a certain sentimentality and loneliness. For over a year she had found herself listening to the rushing noise of New York's volume action and hearing in it the past, an echo of happy times and laughter like a child standing in a haunted room trying to pinpoint the presence of a ghost and having it elude her.

It had been a hard winter but now it was spring and the bitter months of New York cold were behind her. It had rained from sunset the day before, but now it was quiet and after a good night of hard driving she was quiet. She stood there, looking at her reflection in the green-gold river, hung over from a lifetime of parties, men and martinis, and listened to the church bell, feeling her isolation drawn around her like a cloak of despair.

— Well, Carolyn, you're home, goddammit.

38

5

— I beg your pardon, ma'am? Cornell said, placing the martini before her.

— Did I say something?

— You goddamned.

— I'm sorry, she said sincerely. I despise women who swear in a bar. She tasted the drink as Cornell waited and she nodded slightly her approval and then quite suddenly she smiled. Thank you, it's very good.

— And you needed it.

She glanced at her watch, and then looked at him again, smiling again, nodding as she took another sip.

— It *is* lunchtime.

— In New York?

— In New York.

Colonel Sami moved from his table and stood near her. He clicked his heels and dropped his chin in a bow. She turned and looked at him coldly and then back at Cornell.

— May I ask you a question? Sami asked politely.

— If it isn't personal. She continued to look at Cornell.

Cornell backed to the rear counter and folded his arms watching both of them, knowing what was coming.

— Are you old enough to remember the Second World War?

— I remember it, she said.

— Old enough to hate Germans?

She turned and looked at him, studying him a long time, turning back to pick up her drink and sip it, looking at Sami over her glass. She put it down.

— More than old enough, she said.

— We have never met before, Sami said. I have never seen you before, and I dare say, madame, you have never seen me before. I was a German officer—

— You ought to be ashamed of yourself and go out and cut your throat, she said quickly, cutting him off.

Colonel Sami tried to recover. He stepped back and for a moment his mouth was open. He did recover, quickly and held himself erect.

— Have you ever been to Germany?

— I wouldn't go to Germany if it was the last place on earth.

— It already is, madame, Sami said, nodding.

— Self-pity? she asked, looking at Cornell. Or honesty?

40

— The Colonel is trying to rediscover his conscience, Cornell said. It's hard for him to do so. He wouldn't have refused the spoils of war, if he had been a winner instead of a loser.

— Is this a running argument between you two? she asked.

— Pardon me, madame, but I must answer this accusation, Sami said and turned to Cornell. Yes, Harry, but when does a winner seek expiation? He has won. His cause was right. He is proven. His—

— Well now! she said. An intellectual German. Snow me some more.

— I'm not sure I can, madame. You're way ahead of me.

— Most of us are. About three hundred pages.

— The Colonel would like to say he's sorry, Cornell said. He's been trying to say it ever since I've known him.

— Oh, she said.

— But one cannot be sorry for all! He appealed to her.

She drained her drink and looked at him, sucking on the olive.

— Why pick on me? She signaled to Cornell for another drink.

— You're here, obviously a lady of culture and refinement.

— Is that all?

41

— You're here, madame. Close. I do not go to New York often.

— That's the way it is with you krauts, she said. Lean on anything close at hand.

— Why are Americans so bitter against Germany? The Colonel stepped back and became red in the face.

— If you don't know, you'll never know.

— Tell me, Sami asked.

— Wouldn't waste the breath.

The Colonel frowned, looking at Cornell, who was preparing the martini. He looked back at her.

— I wish you would tell me.

— Why?

— It is important to me, for reasons.

— What kind of reasons? she asked. She seemed to be interested and then she shrugged, turned her back on him and lighted a cigarette. No, don't tell me. I don't want to know. I may think about your problem—or even you.

— And that would be a waste of time? Sami asked icily.

— Like drinking martinis. She picked up the next drink and sipped it and then held it up for the Colonel to see. It's all such a big waste.

— Don't judge me. Don't you dare judge me! Colonel Sami declared with a thin voice. Don't stand on your morally secure base of perfect peace of mind if you will not allow me some way to overcome my guilt. Yes! I do have guilt! And if the world will not allow me a sense of redemption, then surely it is mad.

— Who said it wasn't? she asked in her New York voice.

— Then how do I recant? the Colonel demanded.

— I told you, she said. Go cut your throat. You'll feel better afterwards.

Colonel Sami snapped a perfect Prussian bow to her, turned, picked up his hat and cane, and limped out the front door. Terrible entered from the garden and looked at Cornell and then picked up the half-bottle of wine Colonel Sami had left.

— Colonel didn't finish his wine, Mistuh Harry. Shall I put it back and save it?

— No, don't bother, Terrible, Cornell said. The Colonel doesn't feel so well. We might not see him for a day or two and the wine will be flat.

Yessuh. Miz Josephine say she feel better with her wakeup shot and wants a refill, since it's Sunday, and please, suh, now she ready for you to put on the *Butterfly*.

The *Butterfly* reacquainted them with the tragedy of tragic love and the soaring poetry of Tebaldi lightened with the sun and took them away from themselves.

— Another drink, ma'am? Cornell asked.

— Did we judge him? she asked.

— Not nearly as harshly as he is judging himself.

— You like him?

43

— No, I don't. I don't even try to understand him.

— Well, as long as I wasn't thoughtlessly cruel, she said. That's the only thing I can't forgive them for.

Cornell turned and looked at her.

6

It never failed to amaze Cornell when he saw them pouring out of the church, their faces wreathed in a spiritual and dutiful smugness. The bells pealed their cry of deliverance. Men, women and children flowed out of the portals of the church and across the sidewalks and streets of St. Johns Landing and he stood as he always did at his window watching and wondering. Why did they do it? How could they surrender their rights so easily? Yet, even as he questioned, he saw that the concepts of good and evil had given them a choice. On whatever level of low abstraction, they did have alternatives and they did not move instinctually, there was honest sorrow in some and honest pain; he saw Adam Kune with his family, the brood of seven children and the stout wife, walking thin-lipped, hardworking, not at all bitter or resentful. Okay, he thought to himself, take it away from Adam Kune and what does he do? Get drunk? Beat his kids? Isn't this better? It has to be, and it does not matter that Adam Kune is unaware that he did not create the left and the right of it, the good and evil. Let Adam Kune, for all the world to see, a good man, find his few joys out of his great pain. Isn't that his true price—that he can find joy at all? Adam Kune, exaggerated and expanded, is the man in the middle and his struggle is heroic. This deep reflection, Cornell tought, is a mirror image of yourself by any name.

Terrible moved in from the garden, a little more speed in his step. He began fixing glasses, ices and trays.

— Church crowd is in the garden, Mistuh Harry. Little bigger than usual.

— Mockfish must have laid it on this morning, Cornell said. They all have a look of being returned to life.

Terrible laughed and nodded.

— Yessuh, they sure do. The usual free drink on the house, Mistuh Harry?

— That's the standing house policy. Everybody who goes to church on Sunday morning gets a free drink on Harry Cornell.

— Another martini, please, she said. She took a deep breath and straightened her back and opened her suit jacket. She looked straight at Cornell. May I ask what that was all about? She jerked her head toward the garden.

— An infantile war that I started with the local preacher.

46

— Oh, don't you like him?

— It's not a question of like or dislike. He believes in sin, I don't. Yet, though he believes in sin, he doesn't indulge. I don't believe in sin and I'm a sinner running a gin mill.

— Your logic escapes me, she stated.

— It's not important, Cornell said. He refilled her glass and stepped back, leaning against the back counter. She raised her glass to him. Her drinking seemed to have fortified her.

— What this country needs, she said with a scalding mean voice, is instant sin. Vacuum-packed hypocrisy. Clean guilts untouched by human hands. And we desperately need assembly-line integrity that can be had by everyman, in order to counter the availability of easy sins.

She paused and drank the martini straight off. She gasped, but only slightly. It was her third and the effect on her was decided. She lighted a cigarette and leveled her gaze on Cornell.

— I know your type. You live togetherness, colored group therapy. You go in for AMA-approved vices. You hoard cash culture credits. A shoebox full of trading stamps for your very own Picasso. Yes, I know you, because I helped mold your thinking. I come from the big city where we make the decisions and do things like that to people like you. Gimme another drink.

— But I've got antiseptic values, guaranteed by my headshrinker, Cornell said as he began preparing the

47

drink. She jerked up. She did not expect that kind of reply. And I've read all the good condensed versions of the Bible, Homer, Tolstoy and listened to the better parts of Beethoven, Brahms and Mozart.

She smiled and gave him a mock bow.

— You have us, in the big city, to thank for it. But tell me, are you happy?

— When my IBM-rated personality begins to quake a little, I simply dial a prayer—

— For your all-new synthetic spirit, seventy-five per cent nylon.

— and find stainless-steel peace.

She laughed, a good honest laugh, throwing her head back.

— You'll do.

— The name is Harry Cornell.

— What's in a name? she asked, tossing her head negatively.

— It's all a good man has.

— Are you a good man, Harry Cornell? she asked.

— I'm perfect.

— So am I. We should have a lot in common.

— I don't think it would be common.

And then quite suddenly, unexpectedly, overwhelmingly, it was there, flowing between them as easily and as naturally as the sunlight filling the sky. She reacted slowly, and with judgment. She had just had a pass made at her. She knew about such things. She gave him for the first time a good hard look. She shook her head, rejecting the idea.

— Not that, Harry Cornell. How do you know I'm not just passing through?

Cornell placed her drink before her with great care and looked her directly in the eye.

— We don't have any hotels, and one more drink and you're not going to be able to drive.

— 'kay. She nodded, conceding.

— And you're getting stoned, fast. Taking on courage to face something.

— 'kay, it's something. A regrouping into a new position.

— When you start to look for a new position, at your age, it usually means failure, Cornell said.

She snapped her head up and her face hardened, but she softened her voice.

— Or demanding too much.

— Divorce?

She nodded with some difficulty as it hit her and she wasn't sure she wanted to talk about it, but it was out and she let it continue.

— I threw a fit and made the mistake of wanting it all. He was a sweet jerk who didn't have what it takes to slap hell out of me and go ahead with the way things were. You know what I mean, one of those beautiful people who does everything right at the wrong time and I did everything wrong at the right time to make it end on the ash heap.

Cornell turned away, hoping for Terrible to come in and ask for something, sorry that he had opened it up. He never indulged in chatter with customers, except for the most idle comments. He was sorry that he had gone so far.

— Another drink? he asked.

— They took away my merit badges, she said, and for a moment he thought she was going to cry.

— You can stand perfectly still, or you can go on, but you can't go back, he said.

— Don't con me with your homey sentimentalities, she said, raising her head and speaking fiercely. I'm getting a gold-plated, all-fresh, all-new start. Guaranteed.

— St. Johns Landing welcomes you home.

— It better, she said, and there was no mistake in the threat. She slipped off the barstool and stood perfectly immobile, collecting herself. He had seen efforts to straighten up before, and it either went one of two ways: they fell flat on their face or they walked like wooden soldiers. She stood still for thirty seconds and then she was sober. He had never seen anything like it. She picked up her things and nodded.

— Put it on my bill. I'll be around. Harry Cornell, wasn't it? I'll probably become a regular, Harry. And I don't like anything but Beefeater gin and Noilly Prat, seven to one, frozen glasses, and tell that Nazi to stay the hell away from me.

She walked out of The Recreation Hall and a few moments later she drove off, sliding the big car down the street at the same slow, funereal pace.

7

At four that afternoon, when he was getting drowsy and after Terrible had cleaned up, he wondered if he shouldn't take his nap. He hated to be sluggish in the evening and a fourteen-hour day was murder without a break. He yawned, stretched and shifted his left foot to the window shelf, and continued looking out into the street. There were a lot of tourists in town that afternoon, but only a few out-of-state tags that he could see. Most of them came from neighboring towns, out for the Sunday afternoon ride. There wasn't much business in the afternoon and he did not care anyway. He did not want the young crowd and made it difficult for them, demanding to see their drivers' licenses and absolutely forbidding anyone under eighteen to enter. He walked the length of the bar, yawning, and stopped at the stereo and began flipping through the albums. He selected six records, dusted and examined them, and placed them on the changer. The absolute perfection of a Ramiro Cortés chamber concerto drew him closer and closer within himself. The music was unafraid, rich.

— Terrible! he called and walked back to the window. Behind him he heard the garden door open. I'm going to take my nap. Watch the bar.

— Yessuh, Mistuh Harry.

— Lot of people—kids—in town today. Don't serve anyone that can't prove their age.

— I understand, Terrible replied. You going upstairs or home, Mistuh Harry?

He did not answer right away. Delila would be at her mother's and the house would be quiet, but it would not stay quiet. Sunday evening supper found the house filled with his in-laws. He did not like them and they were afraid of him.

— I'm going upstairs, Terrible, he said wearily, and walking back down behind the bar he opened a small cabinet door and very carefully removed a bottle of Nuits-Saint-Georges, uncorked it, and listened to the music while the wine breathed. When the Cortés was over and the Serkin Chopin *Ballades* dropped, he took the wine and a glass and walked to the back stairs.

It was a small room with a large comfortable bed and stereo speakers wired to the set in the bar. No one knew about this, and if anything should come up when Terrible was on the bar Terrible would have to take care of it.

He kicked off his shoes, loosened his belt, and very slowly, looking out of the window into the garden below, listening to the *Goldberg Variations,* drank the entire bottle of wine and fell asleep.

8

He awoke clearheaded. It was a tribute to the good wine. He lay perfectly still and listened to the Cortés again. Terrible would not have dared change his selections. He wondered how many times the records had played through. There were no night sounds. No crickets, no traffic. It would be very late. He was reluctant to look at his watch; that would mean putting on the light and he did not want that, not yet.

He wondered if he might not already be in hell—but in what level of Dante's *Divine Comedy* he could not remember. Lost souls, something—yes. Was he not already dead, and was he not now reincarnating himself? Then he remembered that May first Sunday was Remembering Day. Everyone went out into the graveyards and weeded around the ancient stones and placed fresh flowers for their loved ones. That was the reason for the unusual traffic in town that day. Some of them came solemn, tearful, quiet, grieving for recent deaths, some of them came searching out names of their ancestors as if they needed reassurance of their identity. He could have gone home and not been bothered by Delila and her family, for they would have taken a picnic basket and made a day of it. Delila, innocent and sweet, would be ready to help, eager in fact, moving among the gravestones and taking care of those plots whose families did not come.

Reverence for the dead, the necrophile in man, had always amazed him. But he saw it for what it was; fearing no extension of conscience made man fear his own death. Not wanting it to end, man laid himself barebreasted on the graves of the departed and there it was, conscious of his own betrayal by dumb nature, he hoped to continue.

The Cortés soothed his feeling of embryonic loneliness. It was music taking advantage of life around it, forward, back, easing into new cycles, remembering old ones; the music played out and he got up.

The sympathy with which he indulged himself had often been questioned; but he accepted this criticism. But he could not understand it. Why not glorify the living? Why string out the joys with predetermined concepts that life was something that had to be hoarded and pleasure was the corrupter sending you on a straight line to death? That was the way Delila lived it. And death? A nameless indifference, a condition, a thought, an *idea,* an ultimate preconception of payment of debt overdue since the moment of birth. We live, therefore we must die, and when we die, we no longer have power over ourself. So what? Harry Cornell laughed.

— Fuck it, he said aloud. He went downstairs.

9

The two-two-and-one of five bells ringing on the ship's clock, a small sentiment he allowed himself, one of the few leftovers from his days at sea, greeted him as he stepped into the room. Ten-thirty. Colonel Sami was at his table and Terrible talked with a few customers at the end of the bar. They had probably recognized him from his wrestling days (he had once forced Strangler Lewis to a draw), and Terrible, who got two and one-half per cent of the weekly gross, was explaining his favorite hold, the one-handed half nelson.

— It has to be early in the match, before the body sweat makes anything but bull strength the difference, with the skin dry, like sandpaper—

Cornell glanced around the room, and moving without thinking, picked up a pail and began to water the half-dozen large ferns. He did not speak to Sami and the only sound was Terrible explaining his technique.

57

— A simple hold, early in the match, can do it for you, Terrible was saying. But there is your defensive moves as well, as with the Strangler. I knew if he ever got hold of me it was goodbye Terrible—

— Why did they call you Terrible? the customer asked.

— Because I was.

Cornell smiled to himself. It never ceased to amaze him that Terrible when he talked of his career in the ring spoke with the clarity and articulation of a contract lawyer. The watering finished, he turned to the bar and selected several South American albums, and while they played he prepared and ate a sandwich. The customers left and Terrible turned to show Cornell a five-dollar bill, a tip.

— They weren't sure who the Strangler was, Terrible said quietly. Washington people. They drank a whole bottle of your best scotch.

— You earn your money, Terrible, Cornell said. He glanced over at Colonel Sami. When did he come back?

— 'bout two hours ago. I just gave him his wine and he's like always.

— Go on home, Cornell said. I'll close up. Any calls?

— Miz Pitt, Terrible said, making a face at the name, and Miz Cornell.

— What did you say to Mrs. Cornell?

— Usual, that you had a rush on and was busy with customers.

— Okay. We had a good week. I'll give you your

check tomorrow. Terrible nodded, pursed his lips, and glanced at Sami.

— Don't you ever go fishing any more, Mistuh Harry?

— You mean why don't we go fishing any more.

— I guess I mean that, suh.

— I don't know, Terrible.

— You just sit around here and listen to the music.

— I'm in a funk, Terrible. Call it spring fever. The look in my eye, can't you recognize it? Wanderlust? I used to be a sailor, remember. And I'm not as old as you.

Terrible laughed appreciatively, but Cornell saw that it was not honest amusement.

— What's on your mind, Terrible?

— Nigger like me, I—

— Don't use that word with me, Cornell said sharply.

— I forget sometimes. Terrible straightened and looked at Cornell and took a deep breath, swelling his forty-eight-inch chest.

— What's on your mind?

— Harry, I'll tell you, I'm your best goddamn friend—

— I know that.

— Well, maybe you know some of it then. I got a right to talk to you—

— I never said you didn't.

— Just let me help, if I can, Terrible said.

There was a long moment and then Cornell nodded agreement.

— Okay, you have that coming to you. You'll be the first.

59

— Goodnight, Terrible said.

Harry Cornell nodded and watched as the man walked out of the front door, hearing the pleasantries pass between Colonel Sami and Terrible.

— I'm closing up, Colonel, Cornell said. Finish your wine.

— I went to church tonight, Harry, Colonel Sami said without moving. He began talking as if he were picking up a conversation. The only time I've done that since I've been in St. Johns Landing. Strange experience. I was born and raised a Moslem, of course. A small village outside of Haleb. Westerners call it Aleppo. Sun, dust, flies, dung and disease. One of the biggest diseases was Christianity. And of course the French, who were not just a disease, they were the grace note, a kind of parasite that fed on the disease, and that emphasized the waste of the sun, the choking dust, the omnipresence of flies, the stench of urine and dung. The French came to Aleppo accompanied by pale, hairy-faced nuns and padres with rotten teeth and bad breath and provoked upon us their Christianity.

Cornell moved about the room turning off lights and checking the refrigerator, and listened. Colonel Sami had not moved except to refill his glass and drink it more quickly.

— It is the fear that is injected into the soul by Christianity that I could never understand. Western man seems to need it. I cannot understand it at all. As a boy I was taught to read and write in a Catholic missionary

60

school and of course the price one paid for that was the incessant ritual of the catechism. Intellectually, of course, I understand the split in the sects of Christianity, Catholic, Lutheran, and so forth, but it is all the same, a deepening *spiritual* nihilism by the insistence on the *idea* of a living God. It reminds me so much, your Christianity, of Nietzsche's will to power; self-aggrandizement and that sort of thing. There is very little said in your Christianity about the individual rights. It is all for the aggrandizement of the living God.

— I'm closing up now, Colonel, Cornell said. You about finished with your wine?

— A moment, Harry, a moment, Colonel Sami said. He lighted a cigarette and drank off a glass of wine quickly. Now tonight, for instance.

— I haven't got time, Colonel, Harry said.

— The good Reverend Joseph Chandler Mockfish moved down the middle aisle as though he were a Palatine prince, mounted the stairs and stood in the pulpit and faced his congregation. His voice was low, almost a monotone, and tended to make the parishioners lean forward, straining to hear.

Cornell was amused by Colonel Sami's description of Mockfish. It was accurate, and the one time that Delila had gotten him to go to church in their early marriage, one of those times when he was still struggling to understand his wife, he had come away with a feeling that Mockfish reminded him of the mid-Victorian scientist who was not and could not be wrong.

61

— Mockfish was deliberate, Colonel Sami said, methodical and with a severe composure. Like a lecturer in a university with a forty-five-minute delivery at hand to get through, points to make, and no digressions or jokes, with the attended getting it or not, and carrying on, old boy, just carrying on. There was no preparation, no prayers, just a cold and, if I may say so, a ruthless delivery of Christian logic to induce guilt *and* prepare the faithful for their daily attitude of complete acceptance of sin for the coming week. My dear Harry, it was magnificent. I sat there and could not believe my ears that this was happening. I remember one passage in particular. It was in regard to sinners, the nonbelievers. They, Mockfish said, meaning the nonbelievers, see no further than the world of reality. They refuse to participate, he went on, dear chap, in the glorious simplicity of Christian dialogue. You love, honor, and obey God, and God will love you! *Imagine! You* must *love, honor,* and *obey* God, and in return you only get the *love* of God. One-sided, eh?

Cornell had turned out all the lights and stood at the door waiting for Sami to finish. The Colonel was not finished, and though he drank off his wine, he continued talking after Cornell had locked the door and the two men stood in the darkness of the sidewalk.

— Mockfish did not let his arguments finish there, dear Harry. You keep faith with God, Mockfish said, and God is *there*. There! *Where?* The Colonel waved his cane at the heavens. *Where?*

— Goodnight, Colonel, Cornell said and turned away. Colonel Sami limped quickly to his side.

— I'll walk with you, Sami said. And then Harry, here is the supreme gesture of insensitivity of your Christianity. Mockfish looked down his nose at his parishioners, at his—flock?

— Flock, Cornell said.

— And he continued: There can be no serious argument. Apparently they do argue, Mockfish said, and they refuse to answer the Christian summons—notice the marvelous power word, *summons*, legal, associated with Sheriff Cabell's thirty-eight pistol, ahh! I've seen *that* technique used before. The summons to be a living indulgence of God's design. However, their *arrogance* is no match for the *grace* of God! Then dear chap, Mockfish paused, the perfect timing of an actor delivering the curtain line. *Remember that!* he said. And Harry, it was over!

— Why don't you accept it, Colonel?

— Accept what, dear Harry?

— That you participated in what you know to be pure horror, and then go on with your life?

The Colonel swung his cane around in a perfect arc and stepped back one step, drew himself up. He smiled. The light of a streetlamp fell on his face. The acne scars were pitted holes.

— I will never accept it, Harry. I can't—don't you see that?

— Why not?

— What is the worst thing you have ever done in your life?

Cornell hesitated a moment and then admitted to himself that it was true. It had happened.

— I once rolled a fag in London. I broke his jaw. He died.

— Would you undo it if you could?

— Yes.

— The same with me. I would undo everything if I could, but I can't. It's a question of degree, dear chap. Colonel Sami stopped. He looked as though he might choke.

— A question of degree? Cornell asked quietly.

— Yes, Colonel Sami said, stepping away from Cornell, standing at the curbing and looking into the deep gutter. Relative—yes, the degree. You no doubt had your reason for rolling your London fairy. Money, perhaps— Colonel Sami looked up at the pleasant, starry sky.

— I was broke, sick at the time and desperate. Cornell said.

— And what is my reason? Colonel Sami asked. I am even worse than the true Germans, at least their paranoia is authentic. Mine was, my reason—what was mine? Colonel Sami asked himself. To get back at the French and their insensitive cruelties? Perhaps. To get away from the flies, the filth, the grandmothers who sent their eight-year-old granddaughters out to whore? It all *sounds* as if it would be a good motive. And for a long time I lived quite successfully with it. But I *outlived* it. Ahh! Yes, that is my error. I lived too long, beyond the usefulness of my motives, which no doubt in the beginning were honest and sincere. But now I have no reason, no motive, and if I did know my present condition, I might know where to go—

— To church tonight, to Mockfish? Cornell asked.

— Yes, that woman disturbed me today. Yes, even that, even Mockfish. Yes, I would, for all the holes in your Christianity, I would embrace it if I thought—

Sami again looked up at the starry sky and leaned on his cane.

— I took, too dear to heart, the advice of the Bishop of Carlisle in *Richard the Second: The means that heaven yields must be embraced, and not neglected.* That is what I lived with. And now, I am another character from the same play. Now I am Bolingbroke after Richard has been murdered: *I protest my soul is full of woe that blood should sprinkle me to make me grow. Come mourn with me for what I do lament, and put on sullen black incontinent. I'll make a voyage to the Holy Land, to wash this blood off from my guilty hand. March sadly after; grace my mournings here in weeping after this untimely bier.*

— You have to march by yourself, Sami, Cornell said.

— Goodnight, Colonel Sami said and turned. Limping slightly and leaning on his cane, he walked away from Cornell, who watched him until the figure disappeared around the corner.

10

He was undecided whether to take the car and drive over to Winchester or go home. Delila would be asleep. He did not feel like reading, but he had to go to Winchester in the morning, and the thought of making two round trips was enough for him to head for home. It was then he saw the woman. She had been shielded by shadows. Then he saw she was walking a small dog. She had changed her clothes and was now wearing a summer skirt and blouse.

— Good evening, Cornell said as she approached.

— Good evening. I don't know why, but I had the feeling that you would keep the bar open until midnight, or even later.

— I usually do, Cornell said. But I spend so much time indoors I like to get out when I can.

The dog nosed around his ankles and he reached down and rubbed its ears.

— She knows you. She jerked at her lead when she saw you.

— It's Mrs. Mockfish's poodle. Hello, Spooky. Cornell rubbed the dog's ears again. Spooky and I are old friends. Once in a while she escapes the good Reverend's wife and shows up in my garden and mooches a bite to eat. Cornell straightened up and looked at the woman. Are you staying with the Reverend and his wife?

— He's my father, she said simply. I'm Carolyn Dennison now.

— I didn't even know he had children, Cornell said, genuinely surprised. I thought I'd heard all the gossip there was about St. Johns Landing, but you somehow escaped me.

— My mother died when I was fifteen. The present Mrs. Mockfish married my father after I left.

The dog pulled at the lead and they both stepped off after her, stopping, pausing as she made her inspections.

— When was that?

— No direct questions, Harry, she said wearily. You'll get it all some wet and miserable night at your bar when I'm melancholy and full of self-pity, and have had too many martinis. But it was a long, a very long time ago.

The touch of harshness in her voice he had heard earlier in the bar was there again. In the passing light of a car he glanced at her and he could see the mouth set, and he remembered it was her mouth that had first given him a clue to her character.

67

— I could open the bar, if you would like a drink, Cornell said.

— No, she said. I drink when I want to drink. I'm not in need. Thank you anyway. Here Spooky! Goodnight, Harry.

— Goodnight, Cornell said.

He watched her walk away, a tall, graceful figure, a silhouette against the streetlights, patient with the dog. She did not look back at him and then she was gone.

11

He drove the Winchester Road slowly. The apple blossoms were gone and the full growth of leaves was in. Silent and peaceful, the miles and miles of orchards gave him the feeling of a battlefield after the war had passed. Gravestone-quiet and with a white overlay from the moon, the slightly rolling ground brought back memories of many nights at sea. He was glad now that he had decided to make the trip that night. It was good to get out of The Recreation Hall.

He had been a good sailor. And he had had the character for it. The strict requirements of being able to live with oneself for extended periods of time, taking life as it came, never bothering about the responsibility of tomorrow, all of this had appealed to him and he had responded to it willingly, and he had enjoyed his life.

Why had he married Delila?

He loved her, of course, or at least he had thought he

69

did when they first met, and for a long while after the boy was born. But beyond that he could not find an answer for himself. He had never really given much thought about what his life would be beyond the next trip or the next ship, or woman, or drunk, when and where he would be and how he got there.

His background was as anonymous as his future. He was one of several million of his generation who had caught the tail end of the depression and as a boy had gone right into a war. A male with a name, number and a certain low-middle status in the scheme of society, neither great nor small, not totally unknown, yet not really known, holding for himself certain ideas about dignity and courage, he was Harry Cornell, married, father, stifled, unsure and not a little angry.

But *why* was he angry? There was no specific thing he could accuse with a righteously pointed finger and lay the blame; and he had become a sharpened expert in recognizing when blame was being put off. Delila was a master of the leveled finger and the shrill accusation. He was reluctant to toss off his anger as being the sole responsibility of his wife and *her* frustrations.

He drove on through the clear night and thought about how uncomplicated his beginning in New Orleans had been. One of many boys whose mother and father were chronic Saturday-night drunks, sleeping all day on Sunday, which left them, and this was true as far back as he could remember, Sundays to themselves. Like wild weeds growing between the ties of abandoned railroad

spurs along the Mississippi, boys of all ages roamed the
streets of New Orleans dividing their interests between
the amusement park at Lake Pontchartrain, the river and
the movies. Harry Cornell's gravitation to ships and the
seas beyond was as natural as it was logical with his
limited education and lack of interest in anything but
movies. From the first moment he stepped aboard the
vibrating hulk of a sugar collier running from Tunas de
Zaza, Cuba, to New Orleans, he knew he had found a
place for himself and he stuck with it.

For years afterward he divested himself of anything
but the right to have a good time, and it was a good time
that brought him to Washington, D.C., looking for any
one of the faceless, featureless, anonymous civil-service
girls; it did not matter to him which one and he spotted
Delila. Approaching her at a drugstore counter he
picked her up in ten minutes. Two hours later they were
in bed and as much because of her enthusiasm and
simple, open warmth as anything, three hours later he
was in love. They were married the next day in Elkton,
Maryland. He made one more trip to sea after that, and
when he returned she was in St. Johns Landing, preg-
nant. He was so happy and pleased to have a wife and a
place and a chance to start life all over again that he did
not consider for a moment that he should do anything
but quit the sea and go to her.

St. Johns Landing watched, waited, saw him work out
his life and open The Recreation Hall, and after several

years admitted that Delila had gotten herself a good man.

Everything, he thought to himself as he approached Winchester, would be fine if I could only find out why she's so angry and displeased all the time. But he did not linger over this thought very long. He had made his decision. He was leaving.

12

He parked the car on President Jackson Street and cut the motor. Ahead of him in the streetlight he could make out the name of the cross street: Senator Douglas Avenue. Every small-town chamber of commerce in the area liked to emphasize and point up the historical aspects of the area. There was some confusion in one town nearby when the town fathers had laid out Ben Franklin Avenue with President Pierce Common. The locals called the intersection Common Franklin Pierce and let it go at that. He looked at his watch. It was quarter past one in the morning. He usually did not come this late unless he called first and he wondered if Zach would be still awake.

He approached the door of the gray clapboard house and waited for the dog to bark, and when it didn't, he knew Zach was up. He rang the bell. The dog barked and a few moments later the porch light was turned on.

73

— I don't mind your coming late, but Jesus H. Christ, why don't you call! Zach was a thin, bent-over and ageless man, a confirmed bachelor who had had one good love affair in his youth and escaped, as he put it, and then he settled into his law practice and his reading, which he really preferred over anything else, and took periodic trips to Mrs. Pitt's girls to make his contribution to the livelihood of the Tidewater whores.

— I'm sorry, Zach, but this is important.

Cornell followed the lawyer into a back room that was so disordered that if you did not know the man you would think it was filthy. Books and magazines and an enormous thirty-inch television set; empty glasses, coffee cups, a half-eaten sandwich; and books open, face down, interest in the text insufficient to make Zach continue, but not so bad that he would put the book away or throw it out.

— Drink?

— I'll have a beer.

— What's so important that you couldn't call? I could have had a woman in here.

— You've never had a woman in here. It would ruin your reputation.

— What reputation?

— For being a smart-ass lawyer that saves dirt farmers from losing their place to the bank.

— I have had a woman in here.

— A woman, Cornell said. One. Who was it?

— Never mind.

74

— Your housekeeper.

— Well, now that you press me, yes, it was Mrs. Hyde. But that was seven years ago. Zach passed over a cold beer he had taken from the kitchen refrigerator. What's so important?

— Zach, could you arrange it in such a way, *if* I sold out to Mrs. Pitt and Cabell, that a percentage of the take would go to Delila?

— You leaving, or something? Zach asked, adjusting his gold-rimmed glasses and looking at Cornell.

— Or something.

— Going back to sea?

— I'm not sure.

— You've probably been thinking about this a long time, so I won't burden you with a lot of questions about your being sure.

— I'll tell you, Cornell said.

— I figured you would, Zach said. Delila?

— Partly, Cornell said. He sipped his beer, decided against it and switched to bourbon, moving to the liquor cabinet with the ease of his own home. While he was in the kitchen getting ice, Zach turned on the television set and was watching a B-movie when Cornell returned.

— Why do you watch that garbage? Cornell asked.

— Spend any time in New York?

— Sure.

— Read the *Daily News?*

— Yes.

— The *Voice of the People* column?

75

— I found it a little shrill, repetitious—with rewrites of what the people really said.

— The editing just helped the letters conform to a style.

— You mean they cut out the fucks and shits and goddamn bastards?

— Exactly. But underneath, it really is a part of what we all believe in. A germ of truth, shall we say. It *is* the voice of the people operating. New York is a big city and the little guy can get lost in the shuffle pretty goddamn fast. So, he writes to the *Daily News* and the *Voice of the People.* He gets it off his chest.

— Americana? Cornell asked, half seriously.

— Americana. Not all of us are sophisticated, would-be intellectuals. Most of us are pretty goddamn simple and plain. That's what this soap opera is. Simple, plain. We have a problem. A drunken father, beating the hell out of his kid who wants to be a doctor. Pretty dismal scene. Do you know how often that really happens? So, people sit and watch how the situation is developed on screen and get a lift out of it.

— You're full of crap, Cornell said. I happen to know that this is the only station on the air in the area. You're probably bored to death and turned it on—for who knows what reason.

— You're putting yourself down, Harry. How could I be bored with you as my guest?

— Up yours.

— Thank you.

76

— Can you fix it the way I want it?

— Delila is going to blow her cork, Zach said easily, but with a serious note underneath, meaning it, leaning on it, looking straight at Cornell. You know that, don't you?

— She's got exactly what she wants, Zach. The boy, the house, which is bought and paid for. She doesn't want me. I don't think she ever did.

— Oh, come on, Harry. Don't come busting in here at one in the morning and hang that self-pity crap on me. What is the real reason?

— I'm not sure, but I think I'm bored.

— 'kay. Fair enough.

— Not with Delila, but with most everything in my life.

— You're not a young man, Harry. Not as old as me, but you're not a chicken and you've lived, from what I know about you, a pretty full life. St. Johns Landing after a number of years could wear thin. Ever think that it might be middle-age-itis? It happens, you know. Man approaching that time when he's not quite the man he thinks he is, and then starts running scared, turning to younger stuff, more freedom.

— You mean the promise?

— The promise, yes. Life is a fraud. Don't you know that by now?

— Yes, I guess I do, but when that's so, and you face that kind of truth, don't you do something about it?

— Most of us sit and take it. We don't like it, but we

sit and take it. What's the motivation for doing this, Harry? is it the old complaint? with Delila?

— Delila? No, not really. I admit that I don't like that kind of dishonesty—

— You mean one of Cabell and Mrs. Pitt's parties?

— Yes, and on that point, Cabell accused me of being a moral liar this morning for not getting into the action with him and Chigger and the others.

— What's the reason, Harry? Zach asked, leaning forward and looking at Cornell directly. Why would a sensible man like you throw over what looks to be a pretty good life? You've got a problem with your wife, but that's as common as toothache. It isn't their fault. They're built differently than men, that's all. For ages men have been taking their pleasures out elsewhere. And I know that Cabell is right about you, you *are* a moral liar, but not in the way he means, I know, or at least I believe that you are trying to reach some kind of honesty. The question is, why? Why bother? Haven't you lived long enough to know that there are no neat, set, packaged answers?

— Well, I've already told you that I was bored—not in the sense of being bored but in the sense of nothing-ness—what the hell! I can't explain it to you—

— You came over here to talk about it, so goddammit, try! 'kay?

— I'm not ready to commit myself to anything—don't you see, Zach, that's the whole goddamn thing. We live in a world and a society that demands a commit, right?

— I'll go along, but reserve rights to come back to the point.

— But for now—

— For now, yes, there is a demand to make a commitment. But that *is* organized society, civilization if you will—patterns of conformity, with everybody in a neat hole—the pecking order—

— But based on whose ideas?

— Well, there is the Judaeo-Christian morality—

— Bullshit!

— Well, you may disagree, but it's there. It's a fact, not a conjecture—

— This society, civilization, demands a commit, but what do we get in return?

— Stability. You have to go a country mile to knock it, Harry. It's not anarchy—and there is nothing worse than anarchy. . . .

They drank and they talked, charging in with a new idea before the old one was dissipated, before the old one could be fully resolved, before it could be spoken, drinking and stopping to eat eggs and then back to arguing, getting nowhere, each using the other as a cathartic, purging themselves of emotions and finally getting drunk, but not stupidly, and argued about the colors and mathematical progressions of numbers and powers. At dawn both of them were exhausted. Zach went upstairs to his room and Cornell fell asleep in a chair.

13

The inevitable consequence was a hangover and a phone call to Terrible to open The Recreation Hall without him. Then he called Delila and explained that he was in Winchester on business and would be home later that day. Zach was up and gone by 11:30 when Cornell had dragged himself, stiff and tired, out of the chair to make his phone calls. He took a cold shower, shaved and had one two-inch shot of vodka to help keep the pot of coffee down. At one that afternoon, feeling as though he would win the battle over the headache, he locked the house and took his car over to the block near the bank building and Zach's office.

— Mr. Zachary's gone to the track, Mister Cornell, the girl at the desk told him. He said that you could find him in location eight, but he was only staying for the first two races and then coming back to the office.

Cornell did not feel like going to the track, but neither

did he want to make another trip over to Winchester. The decision was in. He was leaving. And he would have to concentrate on making Cabell and Mrs. Pitt feel that they could make a deal with him, provided they paid the right price. But more than anything he had the fever to leave. It was time, and now that he had made his decision, he knew it was the right one, and he wanted to get on with it.

He drove in the hot Monday heat, getting into the swarm of traffic leading to the dog track, and after a long wait, managed to find a space and hurried to the gate.

The first race was over and Zach had won heavily on a tip from a trainer he had represented in an assault charge.

— I have another one in the second. Same source as the first tip, Zach said as they walked through the damp concrete lobby below the stands where the windows were located.

— I don't like dogs or horses, Cornell said. But I'll go for twenty bucks to win a hundred any time.

— Do you still want me to go through with that thing we *started* to discuss last night?

— Yes.

They did not talk again until after they had made their bets and had made their way to the bar. From time to time they were greeted by friends of Cornell's or Zach's and they had to spend five minutes with a potential client for Zach who had been accused of beating an employee in the storeroom behind the café when the employee had been caught stealing. The potential client had been arrested and was out on bail. Zach said he would take the case and demanded his fee in advance, in cash, then and there. The fee was paid.

— Now get the hell out of here and stay home until you hear from me, Zach told the man. How's all this going to look when the judge hears you're out on bail and out here at the track?

— Weren't you a little rough on him? Cornell asked. After all, you accepted his money.

— This isn't the first time. He likes to use his fists. Ten to one it was some poor high-school kid or Negro who he felt wouldn't go to the cops.

— Will you get him off?

— His brother-in-law is on the county manager's staff. A little pressure here and there—

— Bribe?

— What else? Zach asked in mock amazement. I took his money because I don't like him. Besides, if he wasn't so stupid he could have done the same thing I'm going to do when I get back to the office, which is call the brother-in-law and get the price for the fix.

— You're the most amoral bastard I've ever met, Cornell said with a laugh.

— There are the hounds, Zach said. Our number seven looks like he's got the back-door trots.

Cornell watched as the animal, nervous, high-strung and overbred, pulled at the lead of his handler and stopped to move his bowels. Without breaking stride a dustman came along with a red coat and high hat and swept the dirt into his dustbin. This happened three more times and by then some of the drunks in the stands were making bets that it would happen again. The crowd was roaring with laughter but the dustman never acknowledged them and went about his job.

— That dustman is either a functional idiot or he has steel-plated guts, Zach said. What a way to make a living, sweeping up after a goddamn hound. Well! If I win this little parlay, I'll go home with about six hundred bucks. He lit a huge cigar and rocked back on his heels. Exactly what is it you want me to do, Harry? Want me to negotiate with Cabell and Mrs. Pitt for you? I'll get you a goddamn good price, and I'll only take twenty per cent and protect Delila's interests after you're gone, making sure that she never finds out. No one else, for that matter.

— It's worth more than that, Zach, and you know it. Take a third.

— No, twenty per cent is plenty. Don't worry about me, I'm making a dollar on it.

— At twenty per cent, then, Cornell said. And you take care of everything, including the boy?

— I won't raise him, Harry, but I'll see to things for you.

— Deal?

— Deal.

They shook hands. The rabbit swung around the

track and the dogs flew out of the gates and at that moment he saw her below them. She was wearing a soft pink dress and a big flowered hat. She acted as though she were alone, but he wasn't sure. She was in a box, but sometimes box seats were sold as single tickets on week-days when the boxholder only wanted it for important weekend days and big races. She held a stemmed glass in her hand, high and a little back. Her face was flushed. She pounded her bag on the pipe railing and urged her bet on to win.

He did not, he could not, take his eyes away from her. He was unaware that his and Zach's bet had won; he saw that she had lost, and he could tell this by the way she sat down and finished her drink, tossing it off. He looked quickly at the people in the box with her. Two men and a woman. They spoke, but he got the impression that it was only polite conversation among strangers.

— Six hundred twenty bucks and change to be exact, Zach was saying in his ear. Come on, boy, I'll buy you a drink. You didn't do so badly yourself. Let's see, twenty on the nose and five-sixty to win—nice piece of change. I oughta charge you a tout's percentage—hey!

Cornell was moving away and down to the box. There was a lot of traffic on the stairs.

— I wish I had seen you before, Cornell said to her. I had a tip on the last race.

She looked up, startled, face flushed—from excitement or drinking, he wasn't sure—and then she smiled.

— I probably wouldn't have taken your advice. I hate

inside information. There's such a nagging obligation involved if you win, and you hate yourself for not following your own advice if you lose.

— Heads I win, tails you lose, is that it?

— Something like that.

— Buy you a drink? he asked casually.

— I think not, she said. But thank you anyway.

— 'kay, he said. Good luck on your next race. He started to move away.

— I have my own bottle, Harry, she said, stopping him. She held up a beautifully made leather bottle case. The open neck of a bottle of champagne protruded from the top.

— Oh. He looked at her, not quite sure. Good luck anyway! He smiled and once more turned away and then he stopped, turning back to her, frowning. What did you say?

She looked him in the eyes and waited for a few moments and then she turned away.

— You're a married man, Harry, with a son.

His anger flushed to his face and he felt it pouring over him like hot oil. Was he that transparent? So easy to read?

— I wasn't asking you to sleep with me, he said harshly. Just to have a drink.

— Weren't you? she asked. He saw the mouth set and the face was by now composed, and he knew she was sober. He remembered the way she had handled the martinis and now she had done it again.

— Yes, I guess I was, he replied with much more ease than he thought he was capable of at the moment. I guess I did charge—

— No, you didn't charge, it's just that in a lifetime of dodging passes and nasty situations, you get a certain perception when it's going to happen and you ward it off before the moment of truth—which often produces acute embarrassment. It's not anything special. Every woman has it. I've just got an overdeveloped sense of self-preservation.

— New York, he said noncommittally, almost as if he were reading something in her for himself.

— Goddamn New York, she agreed.

— 'kay, now that we've sharpened our wits and cleared the air of ulterior motives, how about that drink? I'd like you to meet a friend of mine.

— It still goes. You're a married man, and I told you yesterday, I'm getting an all-new gold-plated start here.

— This is a respectable friend. Not a saloonkeeper, not a bum, mostly he's a lawyer, a damn good one, and a good friend. You might need one someday, if for nothing but to protect that gold-plate start for you.

— Why, Harry, you're going to be my friend!

— Not for long. I'm leaving St. Johns Landing.

— Oh, well, in that case.

— What?

— One farewell drink won't hurt, I guess—

— As long as we are chaperoned?

— Right, she said and picked up her bottle case. Might as well get a refill while we're at it.

He stepped back for her to pass ahead of him and she brushed close enough for her perfume to touch at his senses. He sucked in his breath. There was power here, he thought, a raw, honest, tough female power, and his every move up the steps, watching the ankles, hips and back, deepened his instinct to back away from it, to excuse himself and go on home to St. Johns Landing. He had made his decision. He was going back to sea.

But he did not excuse himself when they found Zach counting his winnings and leave her to the lawyer, he escorted her to the bar where they sat throughout the rest of the afternoon and drank champagne and laughed and listened to Zach relate anecdotes about his life in court, with Cornell contributing stories of his experiences at sea and Carolyn sitting between them more beautiful than any woman he had ever seen before.

Before they parted at seven, with the bar closing and the track empty, and walked out to the deserted parking lot, Zach stopped a moment and looked at both of them. He started to speak, then stopped, then turned away without a word, weaving slightly and mumbling something about goodnight to them and slashed out of the parking lot with tires screaming.

— What's the matter with him? Carolyn asked.

— He's moody. He's a frail human being just like the rest of us and maybe a little more so, and every now and then he pauses to take a look at something that he wouldn't ordinarily pay any attention to and it knocks him for a loop.

— What do you think he saw? she asked innocently.

— I think, Harry Cornell said, slowly, he saw us.

— No low blows, Harry, she said quickly, harshly. Keep 'em up.

— We're standing three feet apart, Cornell said. And I haven't so much as touched your elbow! And I don't see how anything can change that situation at all. But there's something here that Zach saw and a smart crack from you doesn't change it, or make it not so.

— Goodnight, she said abruptly and slipped under the wheel of her car and drove away.

He was angry, flushed, excited, light and almost giddy as he drove back to St. Johns Landing that night. When he started to whistle, he stopped and asked himself why he should whistle when he had just arranged to leave his wife and son and was tossing over everything he had worked for, very hard, over a period of years.

Then he smiled to himself and started whistling again. He recognized it for what it was. He was happy. He was not only happy, but he had had a good time. It was heady stuff. He felt silly, but he did not stop whistling even as he entered The Recreation Hall.

— Good evening, Terrible, Colonel. Had a winning day at the track.

14

They did not see each other until the middle of the following week, when she saw him walking down to the river. He has a good face, she thought, watching him from across the street. She smiled to herself. She would have bet anything that she was beyond the time when watching a good man move in the sun would give her pleasure. But it did.

Had Carolyn been aware that she, like St. Johns Landing, was caught up in the speculation about Harry Cornell, she would have denied it. But she had learned almost as much about him as St. Johns Landing knew. And she was pleased and surprised at what she had learned. He was an ex-sailor who had spent many years at sea, touching in on every country in the world with a coastline; he was married to a shrewish woman and had a son; he spoke a flat hard language as if he were still giving orders to illiterate and hardheaded seamen, and he

89

had his own sense of privilege and prerogative. There was about him the feeling of fair field and no favor.

What she did not know about him was that all the time he had spent at sea his luck had been good, and he thought he could transfer his luck from his life at sea to his life ashore. That he had made a mistake in trying to make this overlap was what she saw in his eyes, and the webbing at the corners which tightened like springs when he was thinking about it. She saw betrayal but she did not know the cause of it. She had not only learned about Delila but had made an effort to take a look at her. She put Harry Cornell's sadness and defeat down as stemming from Delila.

With the people of St. Johns Landing it was different. Those who lived near the Maryland panhandle close to the West Virginia line did not believe in good and bad luck, but they knew about pressures. They learned to grope with pressure before they learned to sing their first Jesus song. St. Johns Landing knew enough about him to know that he was a man who had lived a better life than he was then living, married to Delila and running The Recreation Hall. They also knew that Harry Cornell was getting touchy. They looked at Carolyn and decided she was beautiful enough and they sat back in the shade and watched and speculated. Everyone knew about Zach, Carolyn and Harry having a good time drinking at the track. In St. Johns Landing they were very expert in the art of figuring things out and then gossiping about it. That they succumbed to the vindictive streak found in human nature by putting the worst possible construction on what they gossiped about was not known to them and they would have denied it. But it was true. Being bitter, self-pitying and frozen people, they did not like to see a man win. They wanted him to be a loser like themselves.

There were, however, those in St. Johns Landing who had quite a different attitude. And as so often happens when a community or social group unconsciously begins to view a rising controversy, they began to take sides. Those who knew Harry Cornell and liked him for what he was were delighted and pleased at his new vigor and interest in life. Those who hated him, or even disliked him, or even those who only knew him casually, watched and waited for their chance. As a result, Delila knew almost at once that Harry and Carolyn had been drinking after the races were over.

15

— I wish you wouldn't bother with that man Zachary, Delila said. He has a— She made a face, wrinkling her nose —well, his reputation is not very good.

They were having dinner together. Delila called it supper. The boy sat with them. It was one of the few times in months that they had all eaten together. If Cornell wasn't at The Recreation Hall, the boy would be running a fever, or Delila would have one of her sick headaches. He had learned a long time ago that she really preferred that he stay at The Recreation Hall and allow them to have their meals alone. She spoke to her son, changing from the easy softness in her voice to Cornell, to a tender baby talk.

— Just eat a little more for Mama. The child dutifully opened his mouth for the mashed potatoes. He played with a toy airplane, zooming it up and around. He made no noise. He might have been a ghost.

— Zach's the best lawyer in the county, Cornell said. And for Christ's sake, can't the boy eat by himself?

— My papa says there's a very good lawyer over to Hagerstown. A state senator. Now, just a little bit more corn for Mama. That's a good boy.

— You mean Dorrence, Cornell said. He *used* to be a state senator. Fourteen years ago. They caught him with his hand in the cashbox.

— That was never proven, Delila said. That's what Papa said.

— Your papa is senile.

— That's not very nice.

— Sometimes the truth is a painful obscenity. And Dorrence was forced to retire. He made a deal. Cabell told me all about it. So did Terrible. So did Mrs. DuPays. And besides, he said dourly, I need Zach. And besides that, I like him.

— Open up for Mama, Son, Delila said and slipped string beans into the boy's mouth. Cornell watched the routine with disgust, but he held himself. The boy fanned his airplane through the air with a silent preoccupation. Oh, I know why you need him. I heard about his little parties in that big house of his over in Winchester. That's probably what happened the other night when you stayed over.

— You're getting me mixed up with Cabell and Chigger and that other bunch, Cornell replied. And in regard to that, your father once asked me if I couldn't get his juicer into that Saturday night action—

— That's a lie! Delila flared. Papa would never use

93

language like that. Open up one more time for Mama, Son. That's a *good* boy. Look at him, Papa, have you ever seen such a good boy who ate all of his supper? The boy took the last piece of steak and zoomed his airplane.

— Why don't you give him a chance to eat for himself, Delila! Cornell said with anger. When I was his age I was hustling newspapers and shining shoes. And I was running a collection depot for empty booze bottles for several bootleggers and had four kids working for me.

— Hush, please, hush.

— All four of which I could beat hell out of if they got out of line or tried to hold out on me. And not only that—

— Will you hush! *Please* keep that gutter talk where it belongs!

— but I got fried on a bottle of champagne *before* I was his age!

The boy stopped zooming his plane and looked up at his father.

— I heard about champagne on television, Papa.

— You hush up, now, Delila cautioned.

— What does it taste like?

— Ginger ale, only better, Cornell said, looking into the pale eyes and the dead-white face. Impulsively he reached across the table and held the boy's face in his hand. If you were mine, I'd have Terrible teach you how to wrestle and defend yourself, and I'd get you drunk at least twice a year, and as soon as possible, I'd

94

get you laid with one of Mrs. Pitt's nice young
beauties—

— Don't you talk that way to my child! Delila exploded. She leaned over and put both her hands over his
ears.

— He'll probably grow up to be a fag, Cornell said,
sitting back.

— What did you say!

— I said he'll probably grow up to be very sad—that
is if you and I don't stop fighting in front of him.

— It's not *my* fault.

— It sure as hell isn't mine, Cornell said. He closed his
eyes and took a deep drag on his cigarette. He thought
about her. And he didn't want to think about her. He
wanted to think about Delila and his son and he wanted
to enjoy all of the sentimental dreams he had had about
what a life would be, should be, with a family and a
home. He did not want to open his eyes. He saw that he
had for the last few days been staying close to home for
only one reason and that was to avoid the truth about
Delila and the new and growing unease about Carolyn.

— What do you want from me! Delila demanded.

— Nothing.

— Leave the room, Son, Delila said, and the boy
dutifully climbed down from his chair and vanished into
the living room. Neither of them spoke again until they
heard the television set blast forth.

— I know about your going over to Winchester—

— I didn't make a secret of it. I called—

— and seeing that lawyer, Zach, and spending the day at the track drinking with that New York woman.

— Her name is Carolyn Mockfish Dennison, the preacher's daughter.

— I won't stand for it, Harry.

— Stand for what?

— Your flaunting yourself all over this county and making a mockery of my home and my son and my family.

— Zach was with me every minute of the day.

— I wouldn't believe what he had to say on a stack of Bibles from here to Baltimore! *That's* what I think of you and your Mister Lawyer Zach!

Where the hell did it all go wrong! he asked himself, watching her clear the table.

Three hours after the ceremony.

There wasn't anything basically wrong with the boy, except that Cornell realized he had ceased to fight Delila for the boy's attention and love, and *that* could be fixed almost overnight.

— Goodnight, Delila. Don't wait up for me. I may go over to Winchester—

— Harry, please. She stopped clearing the table and looked at him. It seemed that he saw her vulnerability for the first time. She was so pale. He saw, too, her eyes that pleaded, almost like a dumb animal that did not know that it was behaving badly and wanted to please; but he had tried too many times and had responded too many times to those eyes, as they looked at him and begged not to be left alone, to be understood, to be loved. And each time it had failed.

But what could he do? Life went on, was not static. The world moved on an axis that was as pure as the midnight snow at the South Pole. It did not go backward, it did not wait for anything, it went straight, driving straight ahead.

— Harry, please, don't go—down there tonight. Stay with me.

— And if I stay? he asked.

— Harry, please understand, I have a headache—

16

It was ten in the evening and they had moved to the garden. The Saint-Saens breathed magic into their midst. Terrible finally got rid of Chigger, who had been drinking vodka martinis since The Recreation Hall had opened that morning, and after locking the front door, he came into the garden.

— You like something, Miz DuPays, ma'am? Terrible asked.

— One more of the usual, Terrible, if you please.

— Yes, ma'am. And you, Miss Carolyn?

The hot night had driven them into the garden. Zach stuck with the drink he had, Colonel Sami ordered another bottle of wine, Carolyn and Cornell had bourbon and water. Terrible brought the drinks, and, having brought a huge pitcher of beer for himself, sat down next to Zach. The music filled the sweet honeysuckle

98

night. No one spoke. The record played through again. In the distance a mother spoke to a child.

— Harry? A gentle female voice came to them out of the darkness. I can't get Billy to go to sleep. Will you play that piano piece for him, please?

— Okay, Hetty, Cornell replied, speaking up and over the garden wall in the direction of the back yards across the lane. Terrible, would you put on the Schumann?

— Who was that? Carolyn asked. It was so dark they could hardly see each other.

— A friend, Cornell replied.

He heard her chuckle to herself.

— This lovely little town, Mrs. DuPays said in a quivering and thickening voice—a result of her drinking solidly all day long—was fine, and I could live with it and I did, for all these years, until Harry came along.

— Because of the music? Cornell asked.

— Not just the music, exactly—

— I never was much interested in music, Harry continued. I went to my share of concerts, usually after I had drunk myself silly and spent most of my money and had had enough of everything, then I'd go to the Albert Hall, or Carnegie.

— I've always liked music just like this. Unpremeditated, Zach said. I don't know one piece or composer from another. It's all beautiful and I enjoy it when I hear it, but I won't go out of my way—

— I think you're wrong, Colonel Sami said. Music, like a good book, or a good wine, or a fine meal, must be

99

prepared for. In the Albert Hall that you mentioned, Harry, I've seen students and other music-lovers bring the book and sit and listen and read the score with penlights. And at the end, move out of the hall enraptured, as though they were drunk, or full of a good meal. In ecstasy.

— I'm afraid I have to agree with you, Colonel, said Carolyn.

— Don't be afraid, my dear, Colonel Sami said.

Everyone, including Carolyn, laughed. The Schumann came on then, and Terrible returned. The mother's voice came down to them.

— Thanks, Harry. That's the one. That's his favorite.

— Did you go to many concerts? Zach asked of Carolyn.

— Not many, just the ones I wanted, or when I needed something—

— Ahh! I like that, Mrs. DuPays said. Music is something we need.

— After too many cocktail parties, Carolyn went on, too many lunches, dinners, meetings, running from one office to another, I'd just get filled up and I'd go to Carnegie. I'd take off my shoes and I wouldn't move.

— I used to do that in Baltimore, and in Washington, Mrs. DuPays said. I was being courted by a young man in the Foreign Service during the Harding Administration. He was a stuffed-shirt ass, he actually looked like an ass, with long ears and a long face, but he was very thoughtfully in love with me and it was a way to get away from Mama and get out. What I really wanted was one of those handsome Marine officers attached to the various admirals' staffs, and I used Cuthbert to get me around, sometimes three parties in one night. During that time we heard a lot of music, Cuthbert and I, and I felt the need then, just as you described for yourself in New York, Carolyn.

— What happened to Cuthbert, Mrs. DuPays? Cornell asked.

— He cut himself shaving and in four days he was dead of blood poisoning, Mrs. DuPays said. I loved Cuthbert. But I never liked him. I think they say nowadays he wasn't my style, is that it, Carolyn?

— That's it.

— Then Mama got sick and came back here to St. Johns Landing. She was sick for twenty-three years. For twenty-three years I waited to get out and get free, but she just kept hanging on, hanging on. And then when she died and left me all the money, I took a trip around the world and in that time I soon learned that I was no longer young, attractive or ever going to get married again. So I came back here. There, ladies and gentlemen, you have the story of Josephine DuPays. Get me another drink, Terrible, if you please. I haven't discussed or thought about all that in years. Oh, that's not true either. I'm telling a lie. I sit here in your garden, Harry, and I listen to your records and I go over every detail of my life, every concert I can remember, every party I even went to, and I—I—have conversations with people who are dead twenty and thirty years ago. I don't like people who complain about the way things have turned out for them. I don't mind telling a lie, about anything, or to anyone, but not to hurt, only to save someone from being hurt. I guess you would call that my personal morality.

— And it's civilized, Zach said. Quite.

— Thank you.

— A thank-you, Josephine, Zach said, implies that I have done you a service. I have done no such thing. I have stated a fact. You are civilized.

— Don't you turn your legal mind on me, Zach, I know exactly what I am. An old lady drunk who has yet, however, to get falling-down drunk—

— That too, dear Josephine, is civilized. You can't escape it.

— I am *not* civilized. If I had my way I would go up to New York and live in one of the big hotels, taking a suite on the highest floor, and look out over the lights. And drink champagne instead of rye. And go every night to the Copacabana and listen to Frank Sinatra make love to a roomful of women with a song. I love that man. He reminds me of some of those young Marine officers I was after during the Harding Administration.

— I know some people in New York, Carolyn said, who live the way you describe and consider themselves the most civilized, sophisticated people in the world.

— Is being civilized then a state of mind? An attitude? Colonel Sami asked.

— Are you going to drag out that conscience of yours, Colonel? Mrs. DuPays asked. If you are, you're going to make Carolyn mad and I'm going home.

— In the face of such a threat, madame, Colonel Sami replied, I will leave my conscience alone.

— To be civilized, Terrible said, is to enjoy the fruits of a civilization, which by definition is a society or community that has achieved an advanced state of art, science, religion and government.

— Well, Jesus! Cornell exploded. Where did you come from?

Terrible led the others in a roar of laughter.

— If you had whispered that into Strangler Lewis's ear, Mrs. DuPays said, when you two fought to a draw, you might have won. I saw Terrible wrestle that night. I traveled all the way to Veronica, Ohio. I told Mama a friend was in trouble and needed me.

— I know you did, Mrs. DuPays, Terrible said. And I *was* in trouble.

— There being nothing else to say on the subject of civilization, ladies and gentlemen, Zach said, standing up, I will depart. I have to drive home. May I take you home, Josephine?

— That would be nice, Mrs. DuPays said. But only if you promise that you will not get fresh with me.

— I cannot promise, Zach said.

— Good! Always did hate fraidycats. Goodnight all.

The Colonel stood and with Terrible's help they got Mrs. DuPays to her feet.

— I will say goodnight as well, Colonel Sami said.

— Everything is locked up, Mister Harry, Terrible said. He slipped out of the garden and was swallowed up by the night.

17

He knew he was being corrupted. He was a man too well versed in sin, evil, cynicism and negativism not to recognize that he had been seduced by Carolyn's return to St. Johns Landing—an external condition— coupled with his own internal decision to sell out to Cabell and leave, plus the ready acceptance of Carolyn by those who he felt were his friends. It had been one of the finest moments of his life, sitting there in the garden with them and listening to the music. And he could not deny that it was anything but spontaneous. Zach had come over from Winchester to attend to some business and had stopped in for a drink. The Colonel was on his best behavior. Mrs. DuPays had not been nearly as drunk as she usually was at that time of the evening, and then *she* had stopped in, after walking Spooky, for a nightcap and they had gravitated to the garden to escape the loud and obscene Chigger and the heat. There was nothing that he could put his finger on and say that he had helped make the evening by saying this or doing that. It had been Terrible's suggestion to move out of the building. No, he decided, he was going into a state of pure, complete and thorough crisis and all of it had come out of accident and coincidence.

They sat perfectly still and listened to a replay of the Schumann and then Carolyn stood up.

— Goodnight, Harry. This has been the most pleasant evening I've had in a long time.

— Don't go, he said. I have something I want to say to you.

— Save it, she said abruptly.

She started to walk away, to leave by the rear gate of the garden. He reached out impulsively and took her hand. She froze.

— Sit down, please, he said.

— Don't—don't touch me. Let me go.

He let go of her instantly, but she did not move.

— It's been three weeks, he said, since that first Sunday morning.

— I know.

— I told you at the track the following Monday that I was leaving St. John's Landing. As you see, I didn't. And I think you know why.

— Why? No! Don't answer that.

— 'kay, I won't. But we both know. Zach saw it in the parking lot at the track. Now my friends have sat and talked with you and drunk with you here. They like you.

— Conning me?

— No. You've just got a well-turned ear for the con, he said.

— You *betcha!* she said vehemently. I know all the tricks and dodges and turns and little deployments to steal a few minutes and sneak a little love on the side. Oh, don't think I'm above it. God knows, I've been there. But I'm sick of being *evasive,* not only to the world, but to myself.

— Stop pressing, he said. You're not in New York now. You left the five-martinis-for-lunch circuit to come down here for a guaranteed all-new start, remember?

— Snow me some more.

— Don't be rude, he said curtly. Honesty with yourself isn't dug up out of old values, it's found after a long period of painful discovery and getting rid of a lot of old crap! And part of the crap is giving yourself a chance to be decent to yourself for a change, and giving yourself and everyone else a chance at *their* honesty.

— Meaning you?

— Meaning me.

— Don't tell me you're not making a pass at me.

— Of course I'm making a pass at you! he said roughly, hoarsely. But I'm looking for an all new start too! Your bellybutton is not the only center of the universe. I've got a universal beginning too.

He could see her silhouette, vaguely, against the filter of light from the late moon. She seemed to collapse in her chair. She just sat down and with her shoulders hunched over, her hands at rest in her lap.

— It's true. God, it's true. But I've been taken so many times!

— You came down here licking your wounds. You blew it in New York. You let it slip through your fingers. How and why is of no interest to me at all—

— What does interest you, she asked dully, not moving.

— I'm selfish and arrogant enough to believe that when I'm happy, I can make others happy.

— Are you happy now?

— I'm in a state of euphoria. I don't know. I can't read my own reactions clearly at the moment. I know that I've been unsettled since I first saw you.

— Just unsettled?

— What else could there be in this time?

— I'm afraid of involvements, she said.

— So am I, he replied. But those are our hangups. Yours and mine. It does not alter the fact.

— What is the fact?

— That we're here, talking like people with problems to solve and an intense way of going about solving them.

— Are you saying to relax?

— God, woman, neither of us wants to make another mistake. Give it some time. Let it develop and grow, if it's going to grow, let it go where it wants to go.

— And then what?

— You're asking for guarantees again. Some final answer. There aren't any final answers for us, not at this point.

— Maybe what I meant was a promise?

— That we will be together?

— Yes.

— If it's right and true and good, then we'll be together. Neither of us are children.

— That's true enough, she said with a bitter laugh.

— That's the old self-pity crap again, Carolyn, he said. Leave it alone.

— What?

— That you're not a young girl any more, that you've messed up your life so far. You think you're isolated, alone in this area? There are legions of us. You heard what Mrs. DuPays said tonight. Who the hell knows what the real story is—or was—with her Cuthbert? It could be the way she said it was, and it could be an old illusion that she has developed into a delusion to help her get through one day after another. Self-pity. That's the great killer, and particularly now, here, with us. If we don't take advantage of time and see what we have, or might have, letting it come and rise and fall like a tide, easing into it naturally—and if we start pressing, asking for guarantees—then we're dead. You might as well get into your car and go to some other town and find something else.

He drained his drink in one gulp, stood, and went into the bar and poured himself another. He took it straight and then poured another. He was standing behind the bar when she moved into the doorway and stood looking at him.

— I don't want to make another mistake. I couldn't take it, not again.

— Then play the goddamn game, he said harshly.

— And what is the game, Harry?

— I don't know. I don't know, really. I don't. I *think* that it's what I said before, taking advantage of time.

— The great healer.

— And the great killer, the wound-maker, too, don't forget that. There isn't even the guarantee that time will heal.

— You're a hardheaded sonofabitch, Harry Cornell.

— No, I'm not, I'm protecting myself, perhaps like Mrs. DuPays is protecting *her*self, with delusion. And the worst part of it is, I think, I'm protecting you as well. That's *my* crisis. Suppose I go into this thing and find that it doesn't work for me, but it does work for you? You might get hurt. I already care enough to want to protect you.

Across the darkened room he heard her suck in her breath.

— Go home, he said coldly. It's not tonight.

After a pause he heard her move, turning to go back into the garden.

— No, out the front door. We might as well start it right now. He walked swiftly to the end of the bar and snapped on the master switch and flooded the entire room with light. At the door he turned on the overhead sign outside. He opened the door and stood, holding it, waiting for her. Come, he said.

She walked toward him slowly, and it seemed to him that she gained strength with every step, until she passed him and walked out into the street.

18

A huge black limousine was parked in Cabell's Lane and a thin, short, spidery Negro in a chauffeur's livery slowly and carefully polished it with a chamois skin. A cigarette hung out of the corner of his lips. He puffed on it occasionally as he worked; at the sound of approaching footsteps he threw the cigarette away and stuffed the chamois into his pocket. He moved quickly around to the garden side of the car and opened the door; he kept his eyes straight and his back stiff and did not look up as Mrs. Pitt and Sheriff Cabell appeared.

— Time is money, Sheriff, Mrs. Pitt said. This is the last time I'm making the trip. I can't take chances any more, see it? If you and your boys want a party, you'll just have to come to Winchester. It's too long a haul down to St. Johns and it sure, *surely* isn't worth the trouble. Time is money.

She was a huge, obese woman, overdressed in a floppy

hat and a flowered print dress of expensive silk. She walked heavily and cautiously as a person of such size will do. Again and again she nodded her head, agreeing with the facts as she spelled them out to Cabell. The Sheriff courted her with a cautiously appropriate sound in his throat.

— I know you're doing us a favor, Miz Pitt, but—

— Well, the favor's finished. The girls don't like it either.

— We been paying the price, Cabell protested mildly.

— Price has nothing to do with it. She nodded her head, agreeing with the facts again. It's all in the situation. I don't like to operate out of my own back yard— and before you remind me that you're the sheriff, I tooken all that into consideration. I just ain't about to do it any more.

Sheriff Cabell made another appreciative soft sound in his throat and nodded. He looked off into the middle distance. He spoke craftily.

— All right, Charlene, what have you got in mind?

— Business. Me and your kind of business. Let me move in here, into St. Johns with a setup.

— We been through all that before. This is a hard-nosed town. I might make an agreement with you for outside in the county somewhere.

— I don't want the county. I want right here in town. Harry Cornell operates, don't he?

— Harry Cornell is different. A whole hell of a lot different than what you got in mind. In the first place, it ain't illegal to have a bar in this state, or county, and the little money I get off him every week is for nothing more than keeping the small fry down to the county courthouse off his back with fire inspections, building permits and the like.

— You still ain't told me how it was different. Explain me that, or I'm taking this here trip back to Winchester for the last time.

When Cabell did not respond in what Mrs. Pitt thought was a reasonable amount of time, she turned to the Negro and with Cabell's help she was eased into the back seat. The chauffeur moved around to the driver's side and slipped in under the wheel. The car was started and hummed in respectful silence.

— Harry's, well, dammit, he's a sort of hometown boy. Married to a hometown girl, see what I mean? And the town knows him and to some degree I guess they like him. He don't ruffle feathers much. And he's pretty quiet. And on top of all that, everybody's sympathetic to Delila.

— I don't give a damn for none of them reasons, Mrs. Pitt said harshly. He's got them rooms over his Recreation Hall, ain't he? Well, I could put a setup in there that would make a pile, what with all these here field hands working to the orchards. A *pile!*

— I don't doubt it.

— Well?

— He won't do it, Cabell said. He's stubborn.

— Well, I got a message from Lawyer Zachary a few

weeks ago saying that he'd like to talk to me. He didn't say what. But he's Cornell's lawyer, ain't he?

— I think so. Why, what did Zachary want?

— I just told you, I don't know and he didn't say. You got any reason to think that Cornell might be selling out, or something like that?

— No, but you got this thing on your mind, Charlene. Zachary represents a lot of people. Half the knife-fighters and Saturday-night killers I get in my jail are represented by him. That don't mean nothing. Maybe he just wanted some of your new stuff.

— Well, maybe. But what I said still goes. Mrs. Pitt then slid from one massive thigh to the other and eased forward, speaking to Cabell through the window. Lemme ask you this: would them hardnoses you speak about let Harry Cornell get away with it, if it was to happen?

— Probably, Cabell replied thoughtfully, considering what the opposition to such a move would be. But you're barking up the wrong tree, Charlene. He won't do it.

— What's the matter with *you!* Mrs. Pitt demanded sarcastically. There's money to be had and a goddamned good setup to be had. Why, we could make a *pile*, and you just letting it go to waste.

— It's no good, Charlene, Harry would never do it.

— Even if he had to?

— Had to?

— You're a soft and stupid man, Sheriff. Mrs. Pitt

threw herself against the cushions. There's got to be a way to get to any man in the world. You think about it. All right, Slick. Mrs. Pitt rapped the glass partition with a heavy diamond ring. Let's get the girls.

— Now wait just a minute, Charlene—

— This is my last trip to St. Johns. You're a fool, Sheriff.

Cabell stood in the middle of the lane and watched the car ease away and then turn the corner. Sadly, he turned back into his rose garden and sat down in one of the antique wrought-iron chairs his wife favored. Absently he pulled the petals from the nearest rose, crushing them between his fingers and then smelling his palm.

19

— I don't like that woman, his wife said, joining him. There's something slimy about her.

— I don't like her either, honey, Cabell said.

— I wisht you didn't have to have anything to do with her.

— I wish the same thing, honey, Cabell said blandly, thinking about Harry Cornell. But it's law business.

— Oh, look yonder, there's Carolyn Mockfish Denny —or whatever she calls herself now, his wife said, looking off down the lane. She's a pretty thing. I heard her talking to the drugstore clerk this past Thursday and, you know, she's got a tender way.

— What are we eating today? Cabell asked.

— I'm about to fry some chicken. God! I hate Sunday dinners sometimes. Everything is soft and lazy-like and I have to go in there and wrassle with that old stove. I wisht you'd get me an electric one. They got a nice one down to Clarey's over to Hagerstown—

— Chicken's nice, Cabell said.

— And some peas, spring ones, and small seed potatoes.

— Biscuits?

— Pan bread, Mister Cabell. It's too hot to go leaning over that oven today. I'm just cooking on the top. Everything on the top.

— It is a hot day, Sheriff Cabell said, content, pulling at another rose and smelling his palm and watching Carolyn as she walked Spooky. Good God! What a pair of hocks on that woman, he thought. She ought to spread like a summer shade tree. He felt himself stir. He looked at his wife.

— Come on, he said gruffly, standing up.

She looked up and saw his face. Without a word she stood and followed him into the house and began unhooking her brassiere.

— I've got to fry chicken—

— Come *on!*

20

The street was like all other streets in St. Johns Landing, deeply shaded with huge oak and elm. Chigger's house was the only one on the block, which made it perfect for parties with Mrs. Pitt's girls. The limousine pulled down to a stop before the house and Slick hurried smartly to the front door. He rang the bell and stood straight and militarily correct, knowing that Mrs. Pitt would be watching him from the car. He became alert when he heard footsteps and was ready to snap his hat off the minute the door was opened. Mrs. Pitt demanded all of the protocol she had observed over a lifetime of watching movie chauffeurs.

The room inside was bare except for the essentials. With no carpet, there was a faded secondhand look about it that emphasized the empty whiskey bottles, dirty ashtrays, half-eaten sandwiches, discarded clothing. Tom Tyson moved through the kitchen swing door as

Slick knocked again. A man in his late forties, barefoot, he walked gingerly to the door, badly hung over. He acted with the sureness of a man who had done this many times, unhooking the guard chain and opening the door. He turned at once without looking and walked back to the kitchen door. Slick stepped inside and spoke politely, hat in hand.

— Good morning, Mister Tyson. Would you please tell the ladies Miz Pitt is waiting?

Tyson hit the swing door without looking back.

— They know, he said.

The women were getting ready to leave as Tyson walked in.

— We-all got to take this car back to Winchester, boys, Stella said. She looked over at Walker. You know, for a fat man, Mister Walker—I mean, most fat men I ever knew were mean and testy-tempered—but you do right by a girl.

— I plow my furrows, Miles Walker said.

— No, honey, it was my furrow you plowed.

Corinne and Beauty laughed.

Chigger had been an alcoholic since he was fourteen. He was a rack of bones with bad teeth and the chronic lack of depth perception characteristic of all drunks. He reached over to pat Beauty on the thigh and missed. Corinne and Beauty laughed again.

— Party's over, Stella said.

— Party's over, Chigger said with genuine sadness.

— Whyn't you boys come see us to Winchester? Corinne asked.

— We deserve door service, Miles Walker said.

— Well, as f'me, I sure had a *grand* time, Beauty said. It was just gra-und. You don't know how lovely it was.

— I know you had a good time, Tyson said. My back won't be straight for a week.

The insistent horn from Mrs. Pitt's limousine cut their laughter short. No one moved.

— Party's over, Stella said again.

— Yeah, party's over, Chigger said.

— We going to see you boys again soon? Corinne asked.

— Give us a chanct, Corinne. Lordy me! Ain't there nothing that will wear you down? Tyson complained.

— Ah, sweetie, you know what I mean! Corinne said, getting up and coming around to kiss Tyson on the cheek. You did fine. Just fine!

— Well! I hope it's soon, your asking us over again, Beauty said. I like coming up here. It's got a real homey atmosphere.

One by one they turned and looked at her.

— I mean it! Why, this is a *fine* house!

— Come on Baby Face, Stella said, patting Beauty on the shoulder, Mama's waiting. She looked at the boys. Her face hardened into a set mask of pure anonymity, her eyes went blank and her mouth hardened. So long, don't think it wasn't nice.

There was a last-minute flurry as Beauty collected her things and turned to look down at the seated men. She gave them her Five Hundred Watt Smile.

— See you in the funny papers!

The women passed through the door and the men, who had not bothered to look up, continued to stare into their vacuum of space and timelessness.

One by one, Stella, Beauty and Corinne walked with hippity-hoppity high-heeled awkwardness from the house to the waiting car. Their hangovers were further assaulted by the harsh bright sunlight.

— It was a very good party, Tyson said.

— Can't remember a better party, Walker said.

— It was the best, Chigger said.

— The goddamn best, Tyson agreed.

Miles Walker stood, stretched, and walked to the window as the limousine pulled away. A completely uncharitable man, he ran the only successful real estate office in town. He knew every piece of ground, every map and lot number in St. Johns County. A bitterly married man with three children who loathed him, he harbored a congenital hatred for any kind of privilege and authority. This was a leftover from the Second World War. He had been turned down for a commission in the Navy and he still saw the indifference in the face of the superior officer who told him he had been rejected every time he met with what he thought he recognized as the manners and behavior of the officer class. He stretched again.

— Look at this, he said to the others.

— What?

— Come look, dammit, he said testily. It's something.

Chigger and Tyson joined him at the window and stared out into the brightly lit sunny street.

— Carolyn Mockfish, Tyson said, and the New Greek, Sami.

— Yeah, Chigger said. What a good-looking woman that is. That's big-league pussy. Private stock of Harry Cornell's.

— As tired as I am, Walker said, I'd make her holler.

— You couldn't get within a mile of that kind of woman, Miles, so stop dreaming.

— Yeah?

— Forget it, Tyson said. Harry Cornell would cut you into little pieces and feed your fat ass to that little dog she's walking.

— Harry Cornell! Walker said with contempt. What's so hard about him? Tell me that, what's so extra-special hard about him?

— Ask him to his face and he'll show you, Chigger said and laughed, his thin body shaking.

— You know something, Chigger? Walker said without turning, continuing to stare out the window. You're just like all the rest of the ten-cent-store trash in this town. Harry Cornell isn't anything more than anybody else. Nothing special at all. Just a goddamn man—

— But ain't that enough where you're concerned, Miles? Tyson asked and jabbed Chigger in the ribs. What have you got against Harry anyway?

— I don't like him, Walker said. Or anything about him. And neither do a lot of other people in St. Johns. Just remember that.

— What do I want to remember it for? Tyson asked. I've got a head full of nickel knowledge as it is.

— Just you mind what I said.

— Mind *what!*

— Goddammit! I'm after Harry Cornell, that's what! Walker said, spinning around, his face flushed, breathing hard. You wanna make something of it?

— Ahh, you just made that up right now, Chigger said. And you know why?—'cause you got backed up in a corner with your bigmouth talk about that woman. You think you the only stud in town hunkering after her? That don't recognize her for a fine thing? But Jesus Christ, man, it's like looking at a movie star! You gunna get mad at John Wayne because he's got himself a nice relationship with a beautiful woman?

— You can shove John Wayne up your ass! Miles Walker said, his face congested with fury.

— Well, all I know is when Big Jawn hits 'em, goddammit, they stay hit. And between me and you there ain't a hell of a lot of difference between John Wayne and Harry Cornell. I'd hate for that sonofabitch to get mad at me. But *besides* that, Chigger said, cocking his head to one side. I *like* Harry. He's always treated me like a man, even though I know and *he* knows that I'm a drunk.

— You ain't no drunk, Walker said. You're a goddamn alky. A wino. A no-good lush—and you think I don't see that you're putting the good mouth on Cornell because he's married to Delila? I remember you and her. Even back in Cottage School you were sweet on her—

and I bet you still are! That's it, by God! You're still sweet on her—

Chigger moved unsteadily to the table and broke a bottle on the corner and turned to face Walker. The broken jagged edge of the bottle weaved back and forth before the fleshy navel of Miles Walker like a snake's head.

— You fat sonofabitch, you pick up your goddamn socks off the floor and get the hell out of my house and stay the hell away from me—

— You no-good—! Miles Walker started to move, but the bottle came up.

— I mean it, you fat bastard! Chigger said, and he steadied, stood, and the bottle stopped weaving. Now get your lard-ass out of my house and don't speak to me any more anywhere anytime! Harry Cornell serves anybody that comes into his bar, black, white or red, and he gives two full ounces of whiskey for the shot, and he don't steal. Which is more than I can say for you with the way you do business, taking interest and closing money from poor apple-chokers.

— I never stole a dime in my life—

— You're a goddamn liar! Chigger said. Now, either put up or shut up.

— You're both being foolish, Tyson said nervously.

— No, goddammit, I mean it, Chigger said. I may be a drunk, and I may be a no-good and all that, but I don't *lie* about it, and I don't *steal* and then cover it up.

— I'll never forget this, Chigger, Miles Walker said.

— You bet your lard-ass you won't, you sonofabitch. I've had just about enough of your complaining and whining and sour temper. I swear, Tommy, I don't think I ever saw this fat slob smile. Not once. Now get the hell out.

Chigger backed off and threw the bottle to one side, splintering it on the stove.

He began to shake. Walker took a tentative step toward him, his hands balling into fists and rising menacingly. Chigger did not move. He stood defenseless, waiting. His head began to quiver slightly from side to side. He turned his back on Walker and poured himself a drink, then lurched through the back door into the yard.

— Now what in the hell got into *him* all of a sudden? Walker demanded, turning to Tyson.

— Who cares? Tyson said offhandedly. He started out after Chigger, snagging the last of the bottles on the table and walking gingerly to avoid the broken glass. So long, Miles. See you around.

21

— I held off doing about Cabell and Mrs. Pitt, Zach said, after that day at the track. For obvious reasons. The lawyer smoked a cigar. He puffed it several times. See what I mean?

Cornell stood behind the bar at The Recreation Hall and nodded.

— Have you seen much of her? Zach asked.

— Every day, every chance I get, Cornell said.

— I know.

— Then why did you ask? Did you think I would lie about it?

— No, just wanted to make sure that you would understand what I'm going to say to you now. Either do something about her or forget it.

— Say what you have on your mind, Cornell said.

— You can't hide anything like this, you know that, don't you?

— I haven't been hiding. Nothing's happened that should be hidden.

— *I* believe you, Zach said.

— But?

— St. Johns Landing doesn't believe you.

His face hardening, Cornell made a vicious gesture with his open palm, as if cutting a swath with a sword.

— To hell with St. Johns Landing.

— Okay, I agree with you there. But you have to do it clean.

— Meaning?

— Leave St. Johns Landing now, or stop seeing her.

— I just told you, nothing's happened.

— And I just told you they don't have to know everything, every detail. They'll fill in what they want to.

— Something, Cornell said, eyeing his friend, has happened for you to emphasize and then reemphasize your point. What is it?

— How well do you know Miles Walker?

— I know him, not well. Never liked him. Why, is he involved?

— He came over to Winchester yesterday to do some business and saw me on the street. You know they had a party with Mrs. Pitt's girls last Sunday, don't you? At Chigger's?

— So? Everybody knows.

— The way Miles told it, they saw her walking the dog with Colonel Sami. There was some rough talk about her, the usual garbage, and there was a fight—not a real fight, just a threat. Everybody was pretty drunk.

— Who is everybody? Cornell asked, his face tight.

— Tyson, Chigger and Walker.

— What was the fight about?

— You—and her.

— Stop calling her *her*. Her name's Carolyn.

— Hold on, son, I'm on your side.

— What happened?

— Chigger threatened Walker with a bottle—defending you. Walker doesn't like you.

— What the hell is that supposed to mean?

— He can make trouble, Zach said.

— I'll bust that fat-assed bastard before he can take another breath.

— Sure, you could, Zach said. But you don't understand people like Walker. He's protecting himself. You touch him—well! Can't you see it after that?

— What?

— You're the man in the slot. A town like St. Johns Landing? Been here for over two hundred years. Hardly a man, woman or child that can't trace their beginnings back to Washington when he came through here and took Sunday service over at the ruins of the First Church of England when he was a young officer at Mrs. DuPays's place over on her hill—well, there aren't many people that come to St. Johns Landing and disturb the way things are, were, and that they intend to keep. The status quo was established long before the Constitution was written. That's what you're fighting. It isn't

Miles Walker. In any other part of this country they would be running you for governor, and Colonel Sami because of his holdings would enjoy an effortless power. You're not dealing with reality, a pragmatic present, you're involved with a proprietary past, a hate, a disgusting hate. They can't ever get over the fact that it all started here and then went on elsewhere, first to the South, then the war, then to the West. They were left *behind*. I talked to Mrs. Regina Forrest, I had to do something for her legally, and she showed me the *spot*, the *chair*, the *fireplace* and the *bed*, standing in the middle of the room on false legs with a warmer curtain around it, where Thomas Jefferson, ate, sat, warmed himself and then slept. *Not a goddamn thing had been moved!* The woman was *proud* of it. Now, you take an idiocy like that, multiply it a hundred times and several generations, the spawn of that period being Miles Walker, Tom Tyson, Cabell, Chigger, Mrs. Josephine DuPays, and you get an idea of what I'm talking about. They're not about to let you come in here and disturb things. They look at Carolyn and they see every hope and dream and desire they have ever had and *you've got it!* And you don't even belong!

— Have another drink, Cornell said.

— Listen to me, goddammit, Harry. You're intelligent enough to see what I'm talking about. You can't have Carolyn *and* St. Johns Landing *and* Delila *and* your good reputation *and* the rest of your life all at once. You've got to make a choice. These people are desperate.

They'll do anything to cut you down, and by destroying you, they'll make themselves a little more secure that they belong and deserve what has been handed to them.

— I haven't made up my mind yet, Cornell said, stubbornly.

— Well, you better do something fast.

— Is that a threat?

— You bet it's a threat. But not from me. From them.

— I never hurt Delila—

— You think they give a damn about Delila? They care about themselves. Only they have to hide their care, and, in a sense, if I want to be gracious about it, they have been saddled with something they don't want, necessarily—

— That history crap?

— Exactly. You think that everyone has the same sense of freedom and an understanding of choice as you have? You're wrong. They're hungup people. And they hate your guts. Get the message, Harry, baby, you're *on!* Did you know that Cabell is a direct descendant of Horace Cabell, a Revolutionary hero who once saved Washington's life? And that Chigger's family owned everything in sight in St. Johns County? Or Tom Tyson, whose uncle was the sergeant at Burnside's Bridge that kept the men in line? Or that your own wife Delila is a direct, blood relative of William Penn?

— I knew about Delila.

— They don't talk about it around here, because everybody's got something going for them, but you, baby, you're dead! You're what Miles Walker calls ten-cent-store trash! And you're *not* going to walk in and take life, as they know it exists outside of St. Johns, and rub their noses in it. They're out to destroy you *and* Delila *and* your boy *and* Carolyn and anything and anyone else that makes them see that they're blowing their lives with this—this—

— Have another drink.

— You're not listening to me.

— I'm listening, Cornell said. But I'm not going to be hustled. They can take their goddamn history and their injured sensibilities and shove it. They might have to kill me, but that's the way it is. I'm who *I* am, not who *they* are. And if they want to wrestle, well then, we'll wrestle.

— You can't win, goddammit! Zach said. And if necessary they will kill you.

— I never asked for guarantees in my life.

— Is it worth fighting for?

— Carolyn?

— No, not Carolyn! Take her, take Delila, do anything you want, but do it! You can't have it all. They haven't, and they're not going to let you have it either.

— Listen, are you going to have another drink? Cornell asked coldly.

Colonel Sami walked in. Their conversation was over.

22

They walked in the rain. It was the first week in June, with the spring-swollen streams gone, the muddy footing underneath hardened into a firm moss; they walked the Potomac banks and, holding hands, they did not have anything to say to each other at all. When they stopped, standing before an open gorge with a deep spring pool at the bottom, the banks hemmed in close to the water's edge, the dark summer sky mirrored on the surface and disturbed by the rain, she pointed.

— Is this it? he asked.

She turned and stood before him, very close, looking up into his face. Rain-wet wisps of hair were plastered to her forehead at the edge of her headkerchief. She nodded.

— To the exclusion of everything else in my life, this is the one thing I've never mentioned to anyone. In New York, during the hard times, specially the last few years,

I would come back to this place in my mind again and again.

— You'd never find it if you weren't looking for it, he said. You'd walk past it and never know.

He put his arms around her. He felt her warmth through their raincoats, her softness. She allowed herself to be held, close and with complete surrender.

— You seem to have come out of some part of my past, he said softly, looking down into the pool. It's all so familiar somehow.

— I know, I know, she whispered.

— I've had many meaningful things happen to me. Some of them very good and some of them, as I remember it, complete terror. But this is totally new for me, this is something I never knew could exist—not only for myself, but at any time, for anyone.

— What is, my darling?

— It isn't so much that I love, you love, they love, he said, holding her close and looking into her face, but it's the feeling of timelessness—of the depth—

They remained still, holding each other for a long while, the sound of the rain all around them, filling them with a feeling of completion, a sense of wonder and isolation.

They made their way down the steep bank slowly, she leading him, stopping to look back up into his face and laugh, pointing to a rocky foothold she remembered, to describe how she would come to the pool and swim on hot July nights. At the bottom they found a small space at the poolside that was almost protected from the rain by the overhanging thick pine trees above them on the gorge sides. Cornell rummaged around and found small twigs, and with much huffing and puffing by both of them, they got a small, smoldering fire going. The pine smoke tingled pungently in their nostrils and little by little the fire was built until it was crackling and spitting. He pulled out a pint of bourbon and she found three-quarters of a peanut chocolate bar in her bag. They drank and ate the chocolate and smoked and held each other.

The rain stopped. They took off their raincoats and dried them near the fire as they sat side by side and watched the reflection of the flames in the pool. Except for his getting up to go foraging for more deadwood to keep the fire going, they did not move. They remained at the pool until it was nearly dark and then they left.

They were reluctant to leave. They stood, both of them staring into the flames, their dry coats belted and tight, the pleasantness of the bourbon filling them with a warmth unexpected and welcomed, and held hands and did not talk. When the fire had burned to glowing embers, he moved to kick it out.

— Let it die, she said. Don't destroy it. The forests are soaking wet, nothing will happen.

When they got to the top of the gorge they looked back at the faint glow.

— You see, she said in an innocent voice. All that

darkness, and all that space and there we are. That fire—
that's us.

— If you carry your feelings to their logical conclu-
sion, the fire will die—

— Don't say that! she said quickly. No. That's *our*
fire.

— Of course.

23

He had taken to sleeping in the room over The Recreation Hall. Long after Terrible had gone home and there were no more customers, he would play the record machine and stand, with all the lights on, at the window and stare into the dark street. When he was exhausted he would take a bottle of wine and climb the stairs to the room. Often he would not go to sleep until the dawn crept up over the garden.

He would sip his wine and stare into the coming gray day and think and try to sort out the facts as he knew them, and try to understand them, knowing that he had to do something, and not wanting to do anything at all, reluctant to move, content and at the same time discontent. He recognized that he was a man in hazard, and in despair. Through the invocation of his own illusions, he had created for himself, and for her, an overwhelming complexity; that it had all come out of innocence and that his actions had provoked a kind of personal shame further complicated his position, and he seemed to be galvanized into inaction.

He had seen people stunned into inaction with an illusion of reality. He was very well acquainted with purposeful self-made dreams, declaring their intent to be fact while in fact their intent was nothing more than internal decisions.

— Ah, yes, of course, he said aloud.

24

They stood on the Mall and looked up at the Washington Monument. College tourists driving a Porsche with a broken muffler exploded away into the heat of that hot day. They stood very close to each other, she clinging to his arm. Very often she would free one hand and stroke his arm as though she were caressing a cat or a small animal, giving it reassurance and love. He slouched, hands dug deeply into his jacket pockets, and ignored the biting glare of the sunshine. Without a word they moved around to the shadow of the shaft and stood perfectly still and studied the salt-white memorial. Children rolled down the grassy embankment. Mothers in slacks and headkerchiefs trundled after baby carriages and white-haired men and women in free-fitting summer clothes posed for their pictures. All around them the intense morning activity blasted and hooted and husked and belched and swept past, leaving them alone.

They had lunch with a friend of hers in Georgetown. They dined in one of those exquisite garden patios that did not quite roll back the noise of the streets, and that looked like a window display in Altman's. Ann Muggy had been an assistant on one of the magazines Carolyn had worked for and had married a third-rate English diplomat. He was now a copywriter on a trade journal that specialized in the British market. Rake-thin, big-nosed, Muggy delayed lunch a full hour while he talked on the phone. The lettuce hearts were soggy, the meat vapidly warm and the toast damp from the humidity. The sun had moved over and burned the brick yard unmercifully. After the long wait and five martinis Ann, Carolyn and Harry were drunk and headachy. The lunch was eaten hastily without any conversation at all, and they escaped back to Washington, hot, depressed and unsure. They were too late to get into the National Gallery.

It had been Carolyn's suggestion that they take a day together in Washington. She was apprehensive. They sat on the steps of a government building and watched the swarms of afternoon traffic gathering momentum for the suburban rush home.

— Shall we find a nice cool bar? she suggested.

— If you like.

— I'm sorry, darling. Oh, that wretched bastard. He did it deliberately.

— What?

— Muggy. Talking on the phone for so long. He despises America and Americans.

— Then why does he stay?

— It's her money, Carolyn replied simply. And he can't cut it back in England.

— Wrong school?

— Right schools, Eton and Oxford, but wrong connections. Ann's innocent enough. I just thought it would be nice to have lunch there. She's asked me so many times.

— It's not your fault, he said.

— Please, darling, let's start the day all over again. I feel I've hurt you. I never want to do that.

— You're feeling guilty about something that you had nothing whatsoever to do with. And no control over. Come, he said, standing and taking her hand.

— Cold champagne, she said, smiling. In a nice cool bar. Then dinner.

— Not what we did, shall be the test, he said, quoting Emily Dickinson, when act and will are done, but what Our Lord infers we would had we diviner been.

She understood instantly and replied.

— Love reckons by itself—alone—"As large as I" relate the sun to one who never felt it blaze—Itself is all the like it has—

141

25

That Thursday evening they drove for hours, leaving Washington during the height of the homeward rush, getting strangled in traffic, not caring and not talking. At midnight, in North Carolina, they found the place. A large palatial pinewood motel with a dining room and a bar and room service from a main building that radiated out into gravel paths and hidden cottages. They ordered steaks and champagne and turned on the *Johnny Carson show*. They ate and drank and laughed and settled on the couch, she curled up against him and he taking glass after glass of champagne, and they held each other in the casual embrace of innocent content; they both knew; unspoken, they had reached down, down into the core where it was good and true, and there, in perfect innocence, they began to make love. They caressed each other with the mutual tenderness of discovery and despair that it should be gone all too quickly;

yet they survived. Their innocent love and affection, distilled and redistilled, refined even, down to a pure and effortless consummation, was remarkable for its possession of the other as it was demanding. He found her wanton, abandoned, yet with all the richness of conscious awareness; fecund, yet marvelously straightforward and simple. She found him direct, honest, even forthright, accepting him with an incredible deliciousness that withheld nothing and displayed enjoyable, sweet, sweet pain.

They languished in the aftermath, overwhelmed by the truth of their love. It was the one thing that neither could accept without bringing experience and history into this moment.

— Now, she said, we are completely alone.

— Afraid?

— Not with you with me.

— Kiss me.

— This is my very best kiss.

— I want more.

— And everything that I was, and am and will be, is the more for you, my darling.

— Did you know, he asked, caressing her, that I am overwhelmed and at the same time destroyed and at the same time made alive and aware by you, by your very presence, by everything that you are?

— I know, she said. You made me that way.

— How long shall we love?

— Until there is no love in the universe.

— That is only the beginning, he said.

— Where do the fishermen of Portugal go?

— Onto a desperate sea.

— What do they do there?

— They fish for their survival on that rolling sea.

— I am your sea and you are my Portuguese fisherman.

— It is a deep sea, my love, he said. Only the very best are able to make their way in that place.

— You are the best.

— No, I am only a fisherman and each time I go a-voyaging, I make new discoveries.

— I shall always await your discoveries, she said. Make love to me.

26

They stayed the entire weekend. They arose early in the mornings and walked in the forest when it was cool, before the sun had trapped heat in the under-leaf. They walked for miles, stopping to have breakfast from a basket they brought with them. White asparagus, ice-cold Chablis and cheese.

They made love in the forest. They allowed nothing to intrude on them, locating for themselves a place deep in the pinewood and allowing the seduction to rise and fall as naturally as the sigh within the woods rose and fell with a breath of air from the clear blue sky. And when they were not making love they talked, darting, reflective images brought up from the past; long slow un-ravelings of their life before. They explored each other with a hunger to know; curiosity, undesigned, simple and spontaneous, with hurried questions and swift an-swers all going around and around, weaving closer and closer to the rich and full ripeness each demanded now that they were one. They were not disappointed.

In the afternoons they swam and returned to their cottage and made love and slept. In the evenings they dined alone and watched television and drank champagne and made love and talked and found an elastic joy in looking at each other. They seemed to be unable to satiate themselves with the presence and love of one another.

They did not talk about the future. They were trapped in a silken cocoon of adoration and affection and were content to explore the time and place of the present. They did not need anything else and they did not miss anything else.

But there came a time when they understood that it was either over or it was going to continue. They seemed to know, both of them, that Sunday afternoon, that the future was crowding down on them and they had lost a round to time. Both avoided the issue. It was the first dishonest moment between them and both of them allowed it to develop on the blind side: it just wasn't there. They continued as before, laughing and talking even as they packed and started the long drive back to Washington, where she had left her car.

They drove all the way back to Washington without mentioning their days together, or the future. They did not avoid it exactly; it was just something that wasn't there. They listened to an FM station broadcasting a full program of Mozart, she curled up against his shoulder while he drove easily with one hand, face set against the lights of coming traffic. They had to stop once for gas, but neither of them moved and they continued to listen to the concert while the serviceman checked the oil and cleaned the windshield. It was after three in the morning when they arrived at the Washington parking lot where she had left her car.

— Goodnight, my darling, she said, kissing him.

— Goddammit! he said fiercely.

— What is it?

— I feel we shouldn't go back. We should just leave. Shock stunned her as much as the vehemence in his tone. She took his hand and kissed it.

— All that has happened, my dear, she said, pressing his hand to her cheek, is that we have found out we love each other. Thoughtless cruelties, remember? We can always leave.

— What on earth could I do or say to Delila that would make it any easier for her?

— Whatever it is, you must try, she said.

— Sympathy for her? he asked, an edge, unintended, rising in his tone.

— No.

— An agonizing reappraisal of a moral position?

— Darling—

— Does going back alter the facts?

— I didn't mean—

— Does telling her to her face that I'm leaving with you, and because of you, make it easier for you?

— Darling, what *is* it!

— Or do you want or need some sort of personal victory?

She understood immediately what he meant and that she had made a serious error. How serious she was not then—shocked into a moment of near-panic—able to evaluate. But she had been through things like this before. Crisis Carolyn, she thought, out of Stupidity by Dishonesty.

She stalled. She took out a cigarette and lighted a match. You are not without resources, she thought, clinging to the steering wheel with her free hand. She fought to regain her composure, watching him tighten and retighten his facial muscles as he watched her. She read nothing in his face. Nothing. She closed him out of her vision. She cursed herself for being the fool, again, and for being the bitch, again. It had always been that way, she thought. It was like the second movement, a further development of the stated theme in the first movement. One-two! Hadn't that been the *real* truth, not the testified-to, in-court lawyer-truth, of her divorce? It was her move. She thought, selfishly, for a moment and regarded the idea of throwing it all off on him, accusing him of feeling guilty about Delila, but this was soon replaced by a sharpened female instinct to leave Delila out of it. Anything she did now would only drive the point further home. And what was the point?

He's seen through you, Carolyn, she thought to herself. You've blown it. No, there is nothing for you to do, she decided. It's all up to him.

She looked up at him, coolly.

—I don't need or want a goddamn thing from you! Do whatever you want to, she said all in one breath and in her New York voice. She jerked the car into gear and sped off.

He stood at the door of his car and he could still smell her perfume, and, it seemed, feel her very presence in the interior, and he watched the taillights disappear. Miserable, unable to escape from his frustration and anger, he drove very slowly and followed across the Virginia hills.

27

There was no reason at all for him to remain in St. Johns Landing any longer and for three weeks he had Zach searching out and running down potential buyers for The Recreation Hall. But those who wanted to buy could not meet his price and only Mrs. Pitt made a halfway decent proposal. He needed a setup for Delila and the boy, but at the same time he was reluctant to let Mrs. Pitt take it. It was the only thing he had ever created in his life that had meaning for him. And there was a responsibility to the people who had come to regard The Recreation Hall with more than a touch of sentiment. As much for those few who had appreciated what he had built as for Delila he resisted Mrs. Pitt's increasingly attractive offers.

During this three-week period Carolyn and Harry avoided each other. They saw each other every night, but there was no contact. Every night she would come

in for a drink and it would end up being six or eight or
ten drinks and she would get very drunk and she would
sit at the end of the bar and stare at him. Every time she
thought he could hear her without anyone else hearing,
she would curse him, or taunt him, or hiss her hatred. He
never responded. He was stone-faced, held tight and
cold.

— Another drink, Mrs. Dennison?

— I knew dozens like you in New York. You're no
different from the rest.

— This is the last round. I'm closing now, Mrs. Dennison. Having the same?

— You're a liar and a cheat and a *wretch!*

— Closing up now, Colonel, Cornell said, turning
away from her with an absolutely impassive face. You
want another split?

The Colonel looked over at Carolyn and saw that she
was having another drink and shook his head. He held
up a half-bottle of unfinished wine. He would time it to
finish with Carolyn.

If it was not the Colonel it would be Zach or Mrs.
DuPays or Terrible who would remain in The Recreation Hall until Carolyn had had her last drink and left.
Neither Cornell or Carolyn seemed to be aware of their
being chaperoned in this manner.

Cornell had not been home since their weekend and
had moved into the room over The Recreation Hall.
Delila made no attempt to contact him. She knew, as
everyone else in St. Johns Landing knew, about the

weekend. It had been Carolyn herself, now drunk most of the time, who had dropped the hints. Delila knew, as everyone else knew, that something had happened and that the overwhelming passion Cornell and Carolyn had had for each other had cooled into a vibrating, rock-hard hatred. She did not like it, but she bided her time. Time was on her side, she reasoned, and each night she lay in bed and waited for him to come home. The first few days she had been able to cry herself to sleep, great racking sobs as she clutched at the wet pillow and prayed, fighting off fantasies of what she thought her husband and Carolyn were doing in the little room over The Recreation Hall. But as the days slipped by she found it more and more difficult to sleep at all. She dragged around the house uncombed, remaining in her nightgown all day and for days at a time. The only effort she made was to attend to her son. Finally when she was a nervous and exhausted ghost, not washing her face, not cooking, opening a can of soup and heating it, she had the doctor in and he gave her a tonic for her nerves and pills to help her sleep. After the doctor had gone, a neighbor came in and left with a descriptive story of Delila's condition, adding that the woman was wasting away and was indeed dying because of Harry Cornell's flagrant affair with Carolyn. St. Johns Landing, in pretended loyalty to a local girl, burned with scalding disgust and loathing. Zach became alarmed and dared try and find out what had gone wrong between Cornell and Carolyn and why the venom existed between them. Cornell cut him cold:

— What are you drinking, Zach?

— With you, in here, I'm not drinking a goddamn thing, Zach replied heatedly. And you can go straight to hell.

— Take it easy, Cornell said.

— *Take it easy!* You dumb bastard, you're about to get creamed, *creamed!* And you got the damn gall to get flip with me! Zach turned away and walked out of the bar.

— You remind me of a little girl I knew who lived in the streets when I also lived in the streets, Colonel Sami observed casually. We called her Lecka. She was a better thief than I. She was much smaller and faster than I was. In the semiannual roundup of wild children, such as we were, by the authorities, they caught her and put her in a Catholic convent. She immediately ran away. When they caught her again, she ran away again. After a while they stopped trying to catch her and let her alone. I found her crying one night and asked what the matter was. She told me nobody loved her, nobody cared, not even the sisters or the police who no longer came after her.

— You don't know me well enough to talk to me that way, Cornell said.

— Yes, I do, Harry, Colonel Sami replied sharply. But not in the way *you* mean. I recognize a symptom. A condition. It is something that I am very well acquainted with.

Terrible stood in the back of the bar and waited, tense, silent, watching them both. Colonel Sami had not moved. He sat as he always sat, legs crossed, hat on the table, his dark glasses shielding his eyes, sipping his wine and staring into the street. Cornell remained behind the bar, watching Sami fixedly. If he goes for the Colonel, Terrible said to himself, I'm going to have to stop him.

— You're very well acquainted with a lot of things, lampshade-maker! Cornell said.

— True, very true. By all means, let us develop all of the sins, all of the guilts—

— Get out! Cornell said coldly. Don't come back.

Colonel Sami did not move. He smoked his cigarette, touching the ash, and continued to stare out the door. He sipped his wine.

— Did you hear what I said?

— I once told you that I do not allow myself the luxury of a decision, Harry, but I have persecuted myself long enough. I am other things besides an ex-SS colonel. First, I am a man who recognizes that I need forgiveness. That I cannot get it, that is my problem. But I will not any longer deny myself the right to live.

— I'm not going to tell you again, Colonel. You and your business are no longer welcome in The Recreation Hall.

— And part of living, Harry, is making decisions. Do—don't do—go here—don't go. Say this—don't say it. Decisions. And I like you enough to make my first decision right here and right now. And it concerns you, not me. You remind me of Lecka because you are wallowing in self-pity. You saw this woman and you wanted her and you took her and now you are trying to find some way to live with your guilt and your sin and you enjoy self-pity! I know—because *I've been there!*

Cornell vaulted the bar and hit the Colonel, slamming him back against the pool table. Seconds later Terrible threw a short punch that did not travel more than eight inches and knocked Cornell cold.

— God, merciful God! Terrible said as he looked at both men.

28

When he awoke, the lights were out and The
Recreation Hall was quiet. He remembered what had
happened and he lay perfectly still and listened to the
refrigerator compressor kick in. It was the only sound.
Then from the mountains a distant rumble rocked the air
and a flash of lightning, momentarily filling the room
with instant daylight, afforded him a sweeping glance
of the huge room and he saw Terrible sitting at the
Colonel's table staring out into the street. It began to
rain. Walking softly and noiselessly, sliding forward with
perfect grace, Terrible closed the two vent windows on
either side of the door and remained standing staring out
into the street. The rain hit with a sudden and inexorable
power.

— Go home. Go to bed, Cornell said.
— What do you want to do, Mist' Cornell?
— Nothing. Go home. What time is it?

156

— After eleven.

— The Colonel?

— I took care of him. You hit him pretty hard. He was out for about a half-hour. He went home. He paid up his bill and went home. He didn't say nothing. He just paid up and limped out.

Cornell sat up. He felt his jaw. A tooth was loose, and there was a knot on the side of his jaw, near the chin. His head ached.

— Give me a drink, he said. He rose, unsteadily at first and then more surely, and made it to the bar. Terrible moved behind the bar and poured a double for Cornell and one for himself. They both turned to watch the stunning rain wash over the street. A second crack of thunder rattled the glasses and lightning swept in and out, bringing a dreamlike moment of clarity before it was gone. It was, he thought, like his life in St. Johns Landing. In and out. Now that it was over, all the years seemed like an instant. They both drank and continued to stare in hypnotic silence at the rain.

— I had to stop you, Terrible said at last. You were so mad, and you've been holding it in so long, you might have killed him. I did what I thought was best. And I wasn't going to fight you. I just had to put you down. So I did. That's why I hit you from behind.

— It's a good thing you did, Cornell said.

Terrible thought about this a moment.

— Meaning what?

— That you put me down.

— That's what I mean.

— Did she come tonight?

— Yessuh, but the door was locked. She stood there and rattled the door and yelled at you. She couldn't see inside. I was in the back and you was on the floor behind the pool table. After a while she went away.

— Give me another drink. And put on some Bach. The one with the red cover. Not too loud, and make sure the garden speakers are off.

Terrible moved to do as he was bidden and the music issued forth, depressed, soft, as if it were playing on the other side of a hill, but it was a true sound. They drank again and stared at the rain and Cornell let the music enter and he followed the abstractions, and after a while, when the rain was quiet, he was quiet.

— Let it play again, Cornell said when Terrible moved to the machine. Halfway through the second playing, Cornell spoke. That's the first time I've struck another human being since Hamburg. A very, a *very* long time ago. In another world, on another planet, in another time and place, with all the space that lies between from here to there. That's how long ago.

— Hamburg, Germany?

Cornell nodded.

The dialogue on the record was answered, the theme crystallized and the pure emotion in the theme was stated again; then it was gone.

— It was right after the war, Cornell said bitterly, venom in his throat as the memory was caught, held like bloody phlegm and then spat out. I had lied about my age and gone to sea early. Ships to me were like huge angry gods during the war—huge, lumbering things with all the power in the world and because of the war they were wandering aimlessly around the face of the earth, almost as if they were waiting for some inner direction to make them gods again. I clung to the sea, fighting off the war, a tenuous hold on a life I knew would be right for me, if I could only survive. And I put my faith and trust in the gods, those magnificent ships. I was in the war early. I was in on almost every major invasion in Europe. I was torpedoed twice, once in the Pacific and once in the Atlantic. I was bombed in individual actions, by actual count, one hundred and thirty-eight times. I was in the first convoy to Murmansk. I went through it all, clinging to my simple faith in the ships and the life to follow when the war was over, and growing up at the same time. The enemy was anything German. But we, our side, had stronger ideas and once they got a chance to see the difference, why, they would reestablish themselves and become a decent, law-abiding, peace-loving people again. Then the war was finally over and the ships could sail with lights on again and not wander without direction and purpose over the oceans. They could be loving, friendly, purposeful gods again. And one of the first places I went to when it was all over was Hamburg, Germany, with a load of wheat. Ten thousand and two hundred tons of wheat to feed the defeated. We went ashore, half the crew the first night, half the crew to go the next night. Only it didn't work out quite like that. The first bunch got into a fight, a real riot, with some of the defeated lampshade-makers, and we were all restricted to the ship. It didn't bother us too much. There were always ways and means to get a bottle and make a deal to sneak women aboard, and there were plenty of women. Big-boned, round-faced Fraus with kids to feed, simpleminded and idiot-eyed, not knowing quite what had happened to them or their men or their country, but with the same simpleminded-ness ready to accept the conditions and go to bed with any man. A policeman was posted at the foot of the gangway to keep us from sneaking ashore, and we made a deal with him to get women. It was no surprise to us to learn that the policeman had been a major and an aide to a big Nazi general, but there he was, pimping for a few cartons of cigarettes. The women were slipped aboard the ship and every guy had a broad, except that Golden-berg's broad, when she found out he was a Jew, wouldn't fuck. Goldenberg did the natural thing and slapped the hell out of her. She staggered onto the deck and the ex-major came up the gangway and tried to pro-tect her. The woman escaped down the gangway and dis-appeared and Goldenberg invited the ex-major into the saloon to discuss it. But the ex-major wouldn't talk to Goldenberg, for the same reason that the Frau wouldn't fuck, he was Jewish. So I invited him to talk. We went into the saloon. It was about three in the morning. We locked the doors and I stood in front of one and Golden-

berg the other and every time he would try to get out,
screaming like a stuck pig, I would hit him, and spin him
to Goldenberg, or Goldenberg would hit him and spin
him to me. We beat him to death. Two against one, he
said bitterly. That was *their* style.

— Oh, Lord Jesus!

— We took him and very quietly placed him inside
the pier shed, where they found him the next morning.
And that was the last time I ever struck another human
being until, tonight, Colonel Sami.

— Did you get anything out of it? Did you take
anything away from it that hurt you or helped you?
Terrible asked. Jesus Christ! he added bitterly.

— One thing. Just one. It's like India. You don't try to
understand it. It's too big and too confused. That's what
I got out of it. I avoided all critical dialogue on the
meaning of life, my life, and I went straight for the
simple things, and in so doing, I landed here in St. Johns
Landing, self-centered, smug, content but not satisfied.
Then Carolyn came along and I saw that I had been
hiding, playing at honesty, all the while being dishonest,
disgusted, negative, and uninvolved. But I had a commitment—a son and a wife that I had made simple promises
to, and there is no shackle or prison like a simple promise. So I tried to retreat into what was an overwhelming
sense of guilt and find some way to resolve it, an expiation, and the pressure built, instead of easing off, and
I end up here, being no further along than I was as a

young ape in Hamburg, Germany, with the pragmatic difference that I am now an old ape.

The Bach played through. They had another drink and the rain slackened off. The refrigerator compressor kicked in again.

29

The silhouette in the window was Miles Walker watching or sleeping before the television late show. Chigger's house was dark. Her light was on, but though he stood there for a while in the darkness of an old tree there was no movement inside. His own house was dark. The boy's room was only very faintly yellow with the nightlight. He had to look for it, or it would not have been noticed. Down to the river and stare at the deep pools of reflected light from the clearing skies. The rain had brought out all of the perfume and it sifted through to his senses with the sweet muskiness of the rain itself, a raw deep earth smell that was rich with the promise that hidden herbs, roots, weeds, plants, would rise again— the perpetual reflowering. But there would be no reflowering for himself unless he willed it to be so, unless he made a decision. Now he understood dumb nature. It lived on, cycle after cycle without thought, rhyme or reason, and now he was forced to accept what he was, a man of reason and capable of making his own regeneration.

He remained in the streets until it was nearly dawn and then returned to The Recreation Hall and sat before the bar with a bottle and listened to music, alone, attempting to find a resolution within himself, determined to ignore anything but the pulse-beat in his body. He drank himself asleep and fell, sprawled over the bar as the record machine continued to play, contributing to the dead vacuum of nothingness; again and again without reason or purpose, the music filled the room as he slept, contributing nothing at all.

When he awoke the sun was streaming in on him, bright, hot and clear. He knew instantly, as if the sleep had not only aided him, but in fact had contributed to his decision, what he was going to do. An hour later he was driving on the road to Winchester and stopped at a filling station. He was ravenously hungry, but his head was clear. He washed, cleaning his teeth with his finger and gargling until he could at least feel the roof of his mouth with his tongue and returned to his table and ate eggs and ham and drank a whole pot of coffee. In the distance he could hear, and faintly smell, the workers spraying the apple trees with insecticide. Truck drivers, Negro field hands and housewives on the way to shop in Winchester stopped in for gas and a few had a second cup of morning coffee. The sky was clear and a deep summer blue.

— Hello, Cabell, Cornell said amiably, as the Sheriff walked into the small lunchroom. I didn't think you got up until noon. Unless it was business.

— Terrible said he left you in The Recreation Hall about midnight. Where you been since?

— Are you serious?

— I been looking for you, Harry. That serious.

— Why?

— I'm asking the goddamn questions, Cabell replied, easing the weight of his holster as he squirmed into the narrow café chair.

— You're *not* kidding, are you? Cornell said.

— I told you, I'm asking—

— The goddamn questions, Cornell said, feeling the pressure build. All right, if that's the way you want it, I'm not saying a goddamn thing without a lawyer. You arresting me?

Cabell did not answer. He moved slightly and pulled the .38 and aimed it at Cornell's head.

— Your wife's dead. My *pre-liminary* investigation leads me to believe you killed her so you could be with that new cunt of yours.

— Delila! Cornell made a move and Cabell thrust the .38 within six inches of Cornell's temple. Delila's dead?

— Dead. And I'll tell you, Harry, if you so much as smile at me, I'll blow your head off. I gotcha, you sonofabitch.

30

The murder, and Cornell's arrest, became for St. Johns Landing the concern of everyone. Business was conducted as usual. But there was the excitement of it, and since everyone had an opinion, the arguments were many and continuous; the conduct of the people was fever-high and the effect was strange. It was as if the roads had been closed and St. Johns Landing were isolated from the rest of the world, and they alone were the whole encompassing scope of humanity with the power to judge and declare the issues of the case. Legally, of course, this was true, since the trial would be held in that county and the jury would be selected from among their numbers. Yet underneath the fever pitch of their discussions and their arguments, there was fear. They discovered they were asked to make a sacrifice to objectivity and they had never been objective in their lives. Wives were indifferent to husbands, husbands were cruel and loud to their wives; lovers quarreled, as one by one they began to understand the isolation the upcoming trial demanded of them. They were in exile, not only from the outside world and from their loved ones and friends, but they were being hemmed into an isolation of themselves. Reverend Mockfish delivered a powerful sermon on a text from Matthew: vii, 1 Judge not, that ye be not judged. For with what judgment ye judge, ye shall be judged; and with what measure ye mete, it shall be measured to you again. They were undisciplined people and they were not prepared for the consequences of their simple faith and quick decisions. Stung by the realization, they grew angry and were driven into hard, fast opinions; the majority believed Harry Cornell guilty. Not long after the murder and Cornell's arrest the town realized that Harry Cornell would die. There was no hope for him. Let Harry Cornell be handled by the State, by Justice, by the Law. Compassion, even pity, for Harry Cornell, began to appear in conversation and eventually the hatred for him became a silent hatred and no one would say a harsh word out loud against him. Zach watched and listened and waited for the tide to flow in and out, and when he saw and felt this last hardening line of resistance setting itself like plaster, he began to plan his defense.

31

Carolyn's depression reached deep into her savage heart. The last petal had flown into a September storm; it had vanished over a far, far hill and as she watched it she knew there would never be another spring. She resisted all efforts from within herself to get up and carry on. She thought of her denial as truth, and the efforts as the "New York Hustle" leftovers. She felt she had been cheated by the enormous fraud of life as she had been taught to know it and when she questioned if she had ever known life at all she came up with no answers. She raked over the meaning of her existence and stared into the afternoon haze of an early autumn and wiped away tears with the back of her thumb.

From time to time her father and the second Mrs. Mockfish would come into her room overlooking the river and try to persuade her to eat something, and each time she would become silent or speak monosyllabically, offering no resistance to their arguments, but making no move to comply. Her resources were all used up and dissipated in her resentment that what might have been could never be. Her arrogance was the bright hard gracelessness that drunks find in the bottom of a glass, and even this was permeated with dreams, fantasies, defeated infantile hungers, as she daydreamed her way through the hours. She spent her days at the window, her head in her arms, gazing into her private world of a desperate past that had brought her to this. She saw no one and only once did she respond to Terrible, who came and stood under her window and, speaking up to her, gave her the news.

When after a long stretch of day-and-night crying and drinking and surrender, living alone in the room, watching and waiting for each sunrise and each sunset, observing every leaf that fell, when she had cried herself out and drunk as much as she could, and with the first frost sweeping in her open window, she found a way to understand that she was still alive and that she had lost. She emerged into the late-afternoon, flinty sunlight of October and walked down to The Recreation Hall.

The Colonel was at his table, *Butterfly* was playing, and several strangers were drinking at the bar. Terrible served drinks and hurried to her side. It was the first time the Colonel had seen her in over two months and he was stunned. She was heavier, her skin was blotchy, and her hair, combed straight back, was without luster.

She stood inside the door, still, alone, and looked around as if she were lost.

— Would you like to sit down, Miss Carolyn? Terrible asked.

— Yes, that would be nice, she said.

The Colonel rose quickly and assisted her to his table.

— How is he? she asked.

The Colonel and Terrible glanced at each other, and Terrible nodded slightly.

— No one knows, the Colonel said. He will not see anyone but Zach.

— I see, she said quietly. She looked around the huge room. Terrible, you had better give me a glass of something. Wine. A light wine. I'll go straight to hell if I stop drinking cold turkey. I've got to taper off.

— Yes, Ma'am, that's wise, Miss Carolyn.

— How long have I been—drinking? she asked quietly.

— Two and a half months, Terrible said gently.

— Well, I've got to think about my health, I guess. That's a long time to drink. She sighed. Her voice was simple, almost like a child's.

— Yes, Ma'am. Terrible walked to the bar and returned with a glass and a bottle.

— How have you been, Colonel? she asked.

— I am always the same, madame. One day is like another.

— Yes, she said. I've been watching the leaves fall.

— I know, the Colonel replied. I've seen you on occasion when I would take a walk.

— Would you like something to eat to go along with it, Miss Carolyn? Terrible asked as he placed the glass before her.

Carolyn did not answer. She accepted the glass and drank it like water. She held it out for another. She drank three glasses straight off, eased back in her chair, and closed her eyes.

— Don't let me have any more, Terrible, she said in a throaty whisper. I've got to think.

— Anything you say, Miss Carolyn, Terrible replied, glancing at the Colonel.

When she opened her eyes, she straightened her back and without asking, took one of the Colonel's cigarettes, lit it and inhaled deeply. When she spoke, after clearing her throat once, her voice was firm. It was the voice of the woman they had known before.

— Did—he kill her? she asked of the two men, looking from one to the other.

— He has denied everything, Terrible said.

— What is the talk? The feeling?

— The talk, madame, Colonel Sami said gravely, is that Harry killed Delila so that he could be with you. The feeling, well, there is very obvious sentiment in that direction.

— Just exactly what is it he is supposed to have done? she asked in her New York voice and blew smoke out in a thin stream. What are the facts as they are known? She looked at Sami.

— Sheriff Cabell was sitting in his garden about two o'clock in the morning. A half-hour earlier he had seen

THE RECREATION HALL

Harry walking down to the river, but, he says, he didn't think anything of it. Harry often walked around late at night after he had closed The Recreation Hall. I've walked with him myself. It was a hot night. Cabell was about to retire when he heard a scream. A muffled, choked-off scream. He was undecided where it came from and listened intently, he says, for some other sound. He went inside. After he had gotten to his bedroom, he decided to take a look around. He put on his shoes and took his gun and walked up the lane, pausing to listen. Cabell walked toward Harry's house. There was a bright moon that night and Cabell claims he could see, from the street, that the curtains in the living room had been ripped down, the window shade torn. He walked onto the porch to take a look. The door was open, slightly ajar, and he entered. Delila was on the living-room floor, her nightgown torn to shreds. She was dead. Her neck was broken. Later it was determined that she had been violated—raped. Inside the living room there was more evidence other than the curtains that there had been a struggle. There was also evidence of a struggle in the bedroom. She was alone. The boy had been taken to his grandmother's a few days before because, they say, she was in such a state of melancholia and depression she was unable to care for him.

Carolyn took another cigarette and lit it. She leaned forward and ran her fingers through her hair. She reached out and filled her wineglass again. Neither Sami nor Terrible made a move to stop her.

— Why did they arrest Harry?

— He couldn't, or wouldn't, account for his time between midnight, after Terrible had left him here at The Recreation Hall, and when Sheriff Cabell saw him walking near the house. Cabell found him in a café on the Winchester Road early in the morning, eating breakfast.

— Is there anyone else under suspicion?

— Cabell is conducting an investigation, the Colonel said mildly.

Carolyn drank off the wine and immediately poured herself another glass. Sami looked at Terrible but neither said anything.

— It's Cabell then, she said, and his unsubstantiated version of what he saw and how he acted that night?

— That's it, Terrible said.

— And Zach? she asked.

— We haven't seen too much of him, Terrible said. He calls once in a while to see how things are going on here at the Hall, and when I ask him, he says that Mist' Cornell is all right. That's all he ever says. That he's all right.

Carolyn stood unsteadily and closed and opened her eyes. She glared at Terrible and spoke in a demanding, arrogant tone.

— Will you drive me to Winchester to see Zach, now, tonight?

Colonel Sami looked up at her sharply. Terrible

frowned. Her eyes were bright and hard, with a surface shine of the quick drunk.

— Miss Carolyn, ma'am, I don't know if it would be right—why don't you let me call and see if he's home. We might have a long drive over there for nothing. Mist' Zach, he's always tomcatting around—

— We'll take my car, Carolyn said. Come on! Close this place up.

— Miss Carolyn—

— I'll go with you, Terrible, Colonel Sami said.

Reluctantly, Terrible nodded and turned away, going through the ritual of turning out lights and locking doors. Carolyn was impatient. She paced back and forth from the front door to the table with quick, unpleasant facial emphasis as she talked to herself in a mumbled undertone. Twice she stopped at the table and had quick half-glasses of wine which she drank in one gulp.

She took no notice of the Colonel's limp and walked ahead of Terrible and the Colonel, who was breathing hard as they made the slight hill to her garage. She went into the house briefly while Terrible backed the Cadillac into the street and the Colonel reclined in the back. In a moment she appeared in the door and skipped down the walk to the curb and jumped in and slammed the door.

— Let's get the hell out of here! she said harshly.

Three times in the silent drive over to Winchester she opened her bag and drank from a flask of gin. Terrible drove swiftly through the crisp autumn twilight.

32

She was quite drunk by the time they arrived. Terrible had called before they left and Zach was waiting for them. Carolyn did not look at the house or furnishings. She came right to the point, looking at Zach hard and shiny-eyed.

— Did he kill her? she demanded, breathing heavily. *I want to know!*

Zach glanced at Terrible and Colonel Sami, who stood near the living-room door. Terrible shrugged. Sami was quiet as he shook his head noncommittally.

— Never mind them! Carolyn said. Answer the question!

— Hold on, Zach said coldly. You're a little tardy in bringing forth this flurry of action. About three months tardy.

Carolyn stared back at him and sat down without taking her eyes from the lawyer's face.

— Do you represent him?

— I do.

— What's the charge?

— Murder one.

— And if he's convicted?

— In this state, without a plea for mercy from the jury, it's the chair. Zach studied her with the same cold glare he had greeted her with.

— Get me a glass and ice, Terrible, she said without turning her head.

— You know where it is, Terrible. Everything right by the refrigerator. Would you like a drink, Colonel?

— No, thank you.

Zach turned back to her. She was seated, hunched over, her bag in her lap, her face forward, glaring at the lawyer.

— He won't get a fair trial in St. Johns Landing.

— Judge Skipp won't give me a change of venue, Zach said, still cold, still watching her intently. So in St. Johns County, feeling the way they do about you and Harry, that means the chair. Appeal or no appeal. Anything else?

— You're not good enough to defend him, Carolyn said. We'll have to get someone from the outside.

— That's not for you to decide, Zach said icily.

— You show me a legal document where Harry Cornell has consented to your representing him and I'll accept it.

— I don't have to show you anything, Mrs. Dennison.

— Yes, you do, she said, matching his tone and relentless stare.

— May I ask why? Zach asked with deadly calm, swinging one leg over an armchair and flopping into the seat.

— Because you want to get him acquitted, and so do I. And you're the kind of friend who wouldn't stand in the way of that. And you know that I can be of help.

Terrible returned with ice, glasses, water and put them on the table, making room by shoving magazines aside. He retreated to the side of the room and waited. Carolyn removed the flask of gin from her bag and poured a glassful over ice. She took a deep drink as the three men watched her, silently, and waited.

— In what way can you help my client, Mrs. Dennison? Zach asked.

— I had an affair with him. I love him. I'll get on the stand and swear that he was sleeping with me the night Delila was murdered.

— That's an easy lie, Mrs. Dennison. A. D. Benhide, the District Attorney, will tie a roman candle to that one and send it and you straight to hell.

— Harry was with me that night! Carolyn said shrilly. She made an involuntary gesture and slopped half her drink onto her skirt and the floor. She took no notice. With *me*. All night. In *bed!*

— Very interesting, Zach said slowly. That brings it down to you and Cabell. He says he saw Harry, and you say Harry was sleeping with you.

— Tha's right, she said, me and that sheriff-type person. And if A. B. Hidebind can tie a roman candle to my story, are you good enough to put a firecracker under that sheriff? She finished what remained of her drink.

— Why have you avoided seeing me all this time? Zach asked, his tone easing.

— Tha's right. Been 'voiding you, in fac', 'voiding everybody. I been wallowing in self-pity and I been drunk.

— Very interesting, Zach said. Are you sure you didn't kill Delila, Mrs. Dennison?

— And rape her? Carolyn interjected instantly.

— A. D. Benhide is going to love having you on the stand. A woman who had an affair with the accused, who isolated herself because of—what would you call it, guilt?—yes, guilt, that's what A. D. Benhide would go after, and tried to drink her way out of her problems.

— Damn right I drunk.

— It is three weeks until the trial. You should look at yourself, Mrs. Dennison. You'll pardon me, but you *look* like a drunk.

— In three weeks I'll make you f'get you—*any* of you—ever saw me tonight.

— I don't understand, Zach said.

— Health farms, ever hear of 'em? They take drunken middle-aged old women like me and dry 'em out. They sweat off the whiskey fat and massage tone into the flab and—and—

Carolyn stopped and looked around the room glassily.

She took a fresh glass and slopped gin into it and drank several deep swallows.

— Get this! she said vehemently and without looking at anyone. Harry Cornell is mine. He's my life. And nobody and nothin' is going to take him from me. What you think this is, this stinkin' life we try an' live? Somethin' read in books? In a pig's eye. It's I win, you lose. You win, I lose. I lost enough and so has he. It's *our* time to win. To hell with 'em. I hate vi'lence. I never been able to accept it.

Her head was getting lower. She sat forward in the chair and held the glass loosely in her hand, gazing sightlessly at the floor. She raised the glass and drank, shuddered, drank again. She was so confused and loose that Terrible instinctively came forward and took the glass. She offered no resistance.

— I've never been able to even think about vi'lence. Never read books about it and walked out on dozens movies. In my whole, in my *whole* life, I on'y saw it two-three times; mothers slappin' their children, I mean, an' at a cocktail party, once, in New York, two fags threw martinis at each other and started pullin' each other's hair. I puked right there, couldn't even get to the terrace an' puke on Fifth Avenue twenny floors straight down.

She sat up and looked at Zach, but she did not see him.

— How'd I manage to last through all that to come to this place? It's all such a big miserable sickenin' way to be a human bein' an' their promises are for birds an'

puppies an' little girls an' anybody they can get their
meathooks into an' lie an' cheat an' steal an' then they
say be brave an' go!go!go! For *what!* What do you go
for? You go for the lie an'-an' the cheat an' the steal, but
don' let nobody know!

— Of course, Zach said softly. You're absolutely
right.

— Righ'! Of course I'm righ'.

Zach stood and signaled Terrible and they helped her
to her feet. She was limp and yielding. Halfway down
the walk to the car she passed out.

The drive back to St. Johns Landing was swift and
silent. Colonel Sami chain-smoked and Terrible drove
the big Cadillac with an insolent indifference. Carolyn,
unconscious, slumped with her head against the door and
did not even awaken when Reverend Mockfish, along
with Terrible and Colonel Sami, managed to get her
upstairs and onto the bed.

33

Sheriff Cabell had always understood and used fear in others to his own advantage. Even before he was elected sheriff twenty-two years before and he had been a foreman over an apple orchard, he had walked softly, talked softly, waiting for his field hands to reveal some faint glimmer of fear; it did not have to be fear of him, or of their job, it could be anything at all, a sickness in the family, a debt coming due with no money; small, almost insignificant things that he would smell out and turn to his advantage. When he became sheriff of St. Johns County his perceptions were greatly enlarged when he saw the fear people had of the law, a law officer; the power to imprison, to hold, to question— even to kill with a certain impunity. In the twenty-two years he had learned, through his understanding of fear in others, the subtle art of threat; quiet, hushed, and suggestive, he had reached the ultimate in the understanding and the use of power, and not being necessarily a stupid man, he found that the purest art in the use of power was the compromise. Open rebellion against authority, he had seen, could not be put down and leave the holder and the user of power untouched. He had learned this lesson by observing what had happened in Winchester County when the sheriff had gotten drunk and given a savage beating to a high-spirited college student. The boy came from a poor but hardworking family with a small farm. The sheriff did not believe that the family would do anything about it, but he was wrong. The family sold their farm and hired a Washington lawyer, and the sheriff not only lost his position but spent two and a half years in the state pen.

Knowing so much about the application and the uses of fear, Cabell was self-analytical enough and perceptive enough to recognize his own fear, which was to run head-on into trouble or make a wrong move as the sheriff of Winchester County had done, and out of this he had developed the compromise. He hoped for a compromise with Harry Cornell before he had to make up his mind about Chigger. He was absolutely certain Chigger had murdered Delila, and he didn't think it would be difficult to get a confession. All Cabell wanted was The Recreation Hall and everything would go on as before. But Harry Cornell would not compromise. He was asking for, by his refusal to make a deal, a head-on knock-down drag-out fight. Cabell saw that he himself could only come out roughed-up, even if he won.

Sheriff Cabell did not understand it. He held the power of life and death over Harry Cornell and yet the man would not even listen to him. One small gesture on Harry Cornell's part and Cornell could have Carolyn Dennison free and clear, though Cabell could understand it if Cornell no longer wanted her. She had certainly gone to the dogs. He had never seen such a change in a person in so short a time. Delila was dead. Harry Cornell was in a bind because of it. It did not make sense to Cabell that Cornell should try to resist his offer of a solution when there was no alternative.

When he heard about the abortive trip that Colonel Sami, Terrible and Carolyn had made to Winchester to see Zach, he guessed, accurately, that she had finished her drinking, had surfaced, had begun to get a grip on herself. It had been impossible for him to talk to her before this, but now he was confident that he could work something out with her and bypass Harry Cornell altogether. Three days after their trip to Winchester, Cabell decided to test the ground. He waited until Reverend and Mrs. Mockfish were at the midweek prayer meeting and Carolyn would be alone in the house.

She appeared at the door and did not recognize Sheriff Cabell, and this forced him to introduce himself. He looked at her closely, wondering if she might be drunk, but it wasn't drunkenness, only detachment. She was fidgety and stepped back, swinging the door wide, and looking down at the floor, made an abrupt gesture for him to enter. She closed the door after him and he waited, self-consciously aware that he was in Reverend Mockfish's house for the first time. There was the faint musty smell of a house closed and kept clean; the must, he discovered, came from the very old and heavily upholstered furniture. He sat down at her invitation, again a half-gesture, and she sat opposite him. She was freshly scrubbed, with no makeup, her hair was pulled straight back in a somewhat childlike way. She wore a sweater and skirt. In the moment of silence that hung between them before he spoke, he heard the unfamiliar noises of a strange house which the occupant has long since ceased to hear, but in the background of a new silence, each sound was magnified. It was chilly in the room. He imagined the temperature was kept low to save fuel.

Now that he was there, Cabell wished that he had not come. She did not look at him. She sat perfectly straight and adjusted the hem of her skirt to a modest level; she sat back in a position of slight strain, her fingers laced across her stomach and her elbows at an unnatural height, resting on the flowered design of the chair arms.

— I haven't seen you around town lately, Mrs.—ah—Dennison.

— I've been ill, she said, and did not look at him.

— I'm sorry to hear, he said. Yes, sorry about that. But now, are you feeling better? I mean, are you up to talking to me? I could come back later.

— Yes, I can talk, she said. What would you like to talk about?

Her detachment, the vague unreality of her manner, disconcerted Cabell and he had a moment of panic. This was not at all what he had imagined it would be like. There had to be a relative basis of interest for him to introduce his fear, threats and ideas. He was not at all sure he could even communicate with the woman opposite him.

She looked at him and smiled meaninglessly. He smiled back and shifted uneasily.

He was sure now. He should have gone directly to Zach and made his deal there. He had removed his gloves and placed them on the pillow beside him and he reached for them as an indicative gesture that he was going to leave, when she spoke.

— Did you come to talk about Mister Cornell?

— As a matter of fact—

— What is it?

— Well, Mrs. Dennison, I think I should come again. You must be feeling pretty bad, and I wouldn't want to question you when your answers, which could have an important consideration on the case, wouldn't be, well, the best answers you could give, and—

— How can you say that you saw Harry Cornell that night when he was sleeping with me and didn't leave my side the whole night? she asked him, looking at him briefly, and continuing to tug at her skirt.

Cabell froze. He had it all then. The vague detached manner, the fidgets, the seeming inability to concentrate, all of them the symptoms of the serious alcoholic making a painful return back to the world. He could hardly contain his desire to laugh in her face.

— That's not true, Mrs. Dennison, and you know it. I saw Harry Cornell that night.

— You're a liar, she said. I don't know what your motive is, but you're a liar.

— Well, for that matter, Mrs. Dennison, speaking of motives, I know what yours are in saying what you just said, which we both know is not the truth at all.

Carolyn was silent.

Cabell relaxed. He put his gloves to one side. He would be able to cope after all. He breathed slowly and took his time and began to speak in the slow rhythmic manner that he had used so many times before. The invitation of the interrogator to the suspect to confide and speak freely. His voice was like the purr of a jungle cat.

— That being the case, Mrs. Dennison, I ought to tell Mister A. D. Benhide, the District Attorney, and have you jailed as a material witness—

He watched for and saw the spring of fear tighten in her eyes. He continued.

— But seeing that you been sick and all, that *would* be a hardship on you. And I certainly wouldn't want to make your father, the good Reverend, take any more than he's already taken.

Cabell dropped his eyes as if what he was about to say were altogether too painful and indelicate.

— You running around with a married man these past

months, a man accused of murdering his wife so he could have his sexual pleasures with you, tromping around in the woods and going off to Washington for a sneaky—bit of fornicating. Now, I'm *not talking* about what two grown adult people do or don't do. No sir, I leave that kind of judgment to people like your father, the good Reverend. What I'm talking about is, well, a way of getting to the *bottom* of this thing, and *clearing* it *up*, so that it won't be necessary for you to get up on the stand and tell that lie about your sleeping with him and exposing yourself and let A. D. Benhide go after you.

She had ceased to fidget. She was now listening to Cabell intently and with growing horror.

— What could be done to get to the—bottom?

Cabell looked at her sharply. Good God! he thought, she's offering herself. She thinks I want *her!*

— You just go see Harry and tell him to have a little talk with me, and everything can be straightened out.

— And me? she asked, watching him.

— You don't want to get mixed up in this, Mrs. Dennison, he said, purring again. Why don't you go on back to New York?

— New York?

— Just pack your suitcases and get in that fine big car of yours and leave St. Johns Landing, and what you and Harry do afterwards, well, that's your business.

— And all I have to do is to get Harry to have a little talk with you? That's all?

— That's all, Mrs. Dennison. He'll know what I'm talking about.

— What *are* you talking about? she asked.

— That's not important for you to know, he said. You just do as your told. He watched for and saw the resentment and hatred and fear in her eyes and face. He took his gloves and stood up. I'll see that you get in to visit him anytime you want to go. Don't rush it. Get yourself good and steady and stay off the bottle and get to looking like you did when you first came down from New York, eh? You have a little selling job to do to get your stud free and clear. Just convince him he should talk with me and everything will be just like it was before, for the both of you.

Cabell, feeling the full sense and range of his power returned to him, confident and sure, walked over to Carolyn's side and dropped one hand to her bosom.

— And lose some of that whiskey fat you put on. You're a bit hefty.

34

Two and a half months in jail had altered Harry Cornell. After a week of furious hostility, outrage and frustration, which at night turned into grief and despair, he came to accept the fact of his confinement. It was not unlike the imprisonment of being aboard a ship on a very long crossing, seeing the same faces day after day, the utter boredom of a set routine, the limited view of the river, just barely seen from his cell window, to be compared with the never-changing seascape and the complete and demanding discipline and inner restraint.

He had been in many jails around the world, but never for anything more than fighting or being drunk, and never for anything that couldn't be adjusted by a small bail, or fine, or as it was in most cases, a bribe. Being arrested and thrown into a filthy cell was a natural extension of being a sailor. But that had been many years before, and he had been younger, and it had always been looked upon as a lark. He had never liked it and had always been extremely pleased to be released, but he had forgotten about it the moment he was allowed to go his way again.

In the beginning he missed having a drink when he wanted one and he missed the record player and he was still shocked over the death of Delila. He drifted through the days, seeing Zach, aching to learn about Carolyn and his son, asking many questions and never being satisfied with the answers, wondering why Carolyn did not come to see him, why he wasn't allowed to see his son, and literally running The Recreation Hall from his cell, issuing orders to Terrible through Zach. It was such a complete change in character for Cornell that Zach at first wondered about his sanity, but at one of their meetings, pacing back and forth in the small room where lawyer and client were allowed to talk, Cornell explained.

— I learned aboard ship when I was a kid, an impatient kid, that you lived one watch after the other, and you piled things on for you to do, to think about. At three o'clock you did your laundry, but you had made a promise to play poker at three-fifteen in the saloon, so you hurried to get the laundry done and get to the game, then while you're playing, you've promised yourself that at five you would finish that novel you were reading, or get out your sextant and prepare for a star sight, or anything at all to keep you behind time. That was the trick, never let yourself get ahead of time, always rush after it. It gave you reason for going on. It added purpose to the absurdity of your existence, floating around on top of a meaningless, dumb sea. You adjusted, or you were defeated. But each trip, each crossing hardened you a little bit more and it became increasingly difficult to con yourself. A lot of them, sailors, turned to booze to get them past the watches. On a given day, say six weeks ago, when you came to visit me here, I probably had pressing and urgent demands to make on you, right? Well, I couldn't give you the foggiest idea of what those demands were, or why they were so important *at that time!* I am now involved with *other* urgent problems that occupy me *now!*

— Are you saying to me, Zach asked, that none of the things you have asked me to do for you were important?

— Exactly, Cornell replied. It's a way to make the crossing. Nothing more. I am the center of the universe. Where I am, that is where life is. It does not exist anywhere else, except in the mind. I know there is a world outside, beyond the jail, but that is *past* experience. I am concerned with the now. Being a rational man, I must accept the condition, the minute-to-minute life of the now. Nothing else exists.

35

It was a week after Cabell's visit that Carolyn appeared at the door of the county jail and asked to see Cornell. She had not had a drink in nearly two weeks and her technique and knowledge of makeup and dress successfully hid the extra pounds. Her eyes were clear and her voice was firm and steady. She walked with a quick step in the bright autumn sunlight and climbed the stairs to the hundred-year-old red-brick building with the four-faced clock and the silvered dome. The bare hickory trees that shaded the huge and airless rooms in the summer were like gaunt sentinels hovering beside the tomb of a forgotten and oft-misquoted mystic.

Enormously wide boards covered the entire area of the foyer and stairs in back, hand-sawed out of the hickory from the same grove that surrounded the courthouse and jail; the floor was worn down with the tread of a thousand reluctant feet as they approached the brass-railed desk. An aged Negro pushed a dolly as he collected spittoons. The ceilings were twenty feet high and there were wide windows in hopes of capturing air in the summer; the windows were now sealed with tape. The panes rattled. Her footsteps echoed as she walked to the railing and looked up at the uniformed officer.

— My name is Carolyn Dennison. I've come to see Harry Cornell.

The officer stood up and leaned on one hand and pointed with the other and looked directly and sharply at her.

— You sit down over there and wait, he said coldly.

She turned at his direction and saw the wooden church pews that lined the walls and walked over and sat down. The officer never took his eyes from her as he dialed and then spoke into the phone on his desk. She could see his lips moving, but could not hear a word. She opened her bag and lit a cigarette.

— Don't smoke here, lady, the officer said.

She nodded, and turning to look for an ashtray and was startled by a voice at her side.

— I take that, ma'am. The Negro porter stood at her side, smiling.

— Thank you, she whispered, and dropped the cigarette into a bucket.

— You welcome, ma'am, the Negro said and pushed his cart away.

— All right, lady, come over here, the officer said.

She walked to the desk and waited.

— You got anything to identify you?

She handed over her driver's license. He examined it for a long time, turning it over and over. He read it through twice and handed it back.

— You are Carolyn Dennison?

— Yes.

— I'm Allister Dunn, Junior. You remember me? We went to school together.

— No, she said simply.

— In the Cottage School, one Mrs. Denham used to run, down to the river. We was all there together, to the sixth grade. He had not changed his manner or his tone of voice. It was cold, demanding, and his eyes bored into her. She was vaguely aware that he was trying to make her remember. He came down from behind the huge desk and to her side. He carried a huge ring of keys. You were Carolyn Mockfish then.

— Yes, she said.

— And you don't remember me? Allister Dunn, Junior. I lived to the Old Road and had to ride my paw's mule to school. Everybody wanted to ride that old mule. You too, even.

The memory was lost to her. His prodding was the talk of a stranger. His voice, even with his attempts to be friendly, was the same. There was a hardness, a professional authority that would always be there.

— Well, he said as they approached the first steel door. It was me and you and all them others to the Cottage School.

The door was opened and they were in a huge room with bars on the windows.

— I'm sorry, I don't remember.

— I thought sure you'd remember that mule. It had broke wind and Paw saved her for me so I wouldn't have to walk them two miles. But I had to take care of her. And I did. I cried when Rhoda died. Good ol' mule, and you don't remember, but you rode her many times in the schoolyard during recess.

— I'm sorry, she said.

— This here is the courtroom, the officer said. We use it for elections. That's why you don't see a big fancy desk for the judge to sit, or a jury box. We move in tables and chairs and use them church pews back yonder for the jury. There's a log of history in this room.

He pointed to one of several doors off the huge room and they stopped before it while he selected a key and opened it.

— This is the lawyer's room. I'll bring the prisoner here. You have to leave your pocketbook and any presents for the prisoner here on this table. Nobody is going to touch them. There's a buzzer inside. You push that when you want to leave. Sheriff Cabell said to give you all the time you wanted.

— Thank you, Mister Dunn. I'm sorry that I don't remember you or your mule. But I do remember the Cottage School—

— That's all right, he said in the same voice. I know you been to New York, and that you got a lot of trouble right now. But there's a lot of us here to St. Johns Landing that remember you. You were the smartest and prettiest girl in the Cottage School.

— Thank you, she said.

— I guess the thing I remember most about you, the officer said, pausing, looking off at the dying sunlight through the barred windows, fingering the keys, is that you had a lunch brought you every day by your Mammy cook. Sometimes even Reverend Mockfish himself would come.

— Did I? she asked.

— Yes, ma'am. That's one of the ways I used to be able to eat, was letting you ride Rhoda for some of your lunch.

She remembered then. A thin, scrawny boy in overalls and long legs and dirty feet who chewed his pencil.

— It was a good trade, she said quietly. They always brought me too much to eat. I remember your mule now.

He smiled and surprised her with white, even teeth. Then she remembered it all in a flash. There was talk, gossip among the children that he was part Indian. She saw now that he was. The teeth. Any man from that part of the country at the age of forty or more wouldn't have teeth like that unless he was Indian.

— Yes, ma'am, he said awkwardly. Now you just go in and sit down and I'll go get Harry—I mean, the prisoner.

— Thank you.

She entered and turned, startled at the click of the door. It had not occurred to her that she would be locked inside. There were two chairs and a table. The floor was scrubbed to a yellow-white and there was the strong odor of disinfectant. A single barred window looked out over an inner court. From wall to wall the court was paved with concrete, and tar had been laced into the seams to keep it from cracking at the edges. At one end of the court a high wall with broken glass embedded in the top gave her a view of the sky and the stark winter hickory trees. The room and the court had no relationship to life, and she was reminded of the castle prisons she had seen in Europe, perfectly designed for their purpose of keeping prisoners confined; simple, pure, as marvelously functional as the wheel.

She was looking out of the window when the door opened and she heard him enter; the door was closed. Neither of them moved. She could hear his breathing.

— Hello, darling, she said without turning around.

— Hello, Carolyn, he said.

— In your cell, where they keep you, can you see the sky?

— Yes.

— And the trees?

— Yes.

— I—I don't want to turn around. I'm afraid for you to see me, she said quietly. I've been drinking. I'm not very beautiful.

— Zach told me, he said.

— Yes—Zach would have told you. He's a good friend.

— Why did you come, Carolyn? Cornell asked.

— I thought it was time, and I didn't want to leave it incomplete.

— Leave *us* incomplete?

She turned then and looked at him. He was thinner. His face was drawn and she could see a very sharp jawline. He was pale—prison pallor, the phrase startled her—and he was not like himself at all. A slight fleshiness from his drinking, that had softened his features, was gone.

— Yes, leave us incomplete.

— I'm in jail, about to go on trial for my life; that's about as complete as you can get. He moved, slipping forward noiselessly, and she noticed he was wearing slippers. He sat on the edge of the table and looked at her. He waited.

— Do you want me to go? she asked. When he didn't answer she sighed. You have every right to be bitter.

— Guilty, perhaps. Guilty as hell, but not bitter. And you sound like a sentimental drunk quoting soap opera.

He watched her for a moment and then turned away, pulling out a package of cigarettes and lighting one.

— May I have one? They took mine away.

He gave her a cigarette and when she came close to him for the light, he could smell her perfume. He closed his eyes and broke away, spinning off the table and putting it between them. He stared out of the window.

198

From that angle he could only see a portion of the cellblock opposite, and not any of the sky or the trees.

— And my guilt? she said plaintively.

— What are you guilty of? I don't see that you have a problem. You can go home and get drunk and forget it, or you can get in your car and go away, back to New York.

— I have my decisions to make too, she said firmly.

— Then make them without consulting me.

— I love you, she said simply.

— Stop it! he said.

— And I will always love you.

— I'm your current fix, your placebo.

She did not reply for a long time and they both looked out of the window. After a while he got up and walked to the door and raised his hand to ring the buzzer.

— Please! Don't! Not yet.

— Why not? We've seen each other. You can go away now with a sense of completeness.

— Please, she pleaded, don't use sarcasm on me. Don't hit me any more. I can't take it. I can't— Her voice became hoarse and sandpapery. I can't take it any more. I want to be less sure, less confident, less competitive. I want to get fat and have babies and slop around the house in the mornings in a housecoat and welcome you home when you've returned from work and take you to bed and smother you with affection and warmth in two big flaccid breasts and hold you and let my warmth and my *self*, my being, give you courage to go away again in the morning—and I don't want to expect anything, anything at all in return but that you will come back to me.

She began to cry. Silently. Looking up at the window.

— That's a demand in itself, he said. Suppose I didn't want that? Suppose I wanted you as you were. A big-league blonde, marvelously smelly and perfumy and a swinger?

She continued to cry.

— Please, oh God, please, come hold me.

— Do you want me or are you rebelling against your failure, your destruction in New York?

— Please—*please* don't be like that. I *can't* take it. God, I'm so vulnerable. Can't you see, darling? I came home looking for a sense of belonging and—and truth, a beginning. But I wanted it on the old terms—New York terms. I still had illusions as to what constituted, what created living—what was life itself. Now—I see—now, now I see that it's being a woman for a man. With no restrictions. If he wants eggs, give him eggs. If he wants children, give him children. If he wants—he wants to go to bed, go to bed. If he wants to fly to the moon, *goddammit!* You get out in the back yard and flap your goddamn arms!

She broke and began to sob hysterically. She reached out for the support of the wall and misjudged the distance and staggered. Her makeup began to run down her cheeks. He stood as if made of stone and listened to her, compressed lids, compressed lips, grinding teeth, and turned away and reached for the buzzer again.

— Oh, God, God, please don't. Don't. I beg of you. Don't. I didn't mean to betray what we had. Can't you see that. I didn't *know!* When I hurt you it was in innocent hurt—a thoughtless cruelty—but I know now. I know, and I understand, I *do!* what it's all about. And I do, oh, God, please believe me, I do know that I love you.

She broke again into hysterical sobbing, groping for one of the chairs and collapsing into it, then gradually slumping until her head rested on the arm. He stood, and watched her.

36

He did not know how much time had passed. He had sat down in the other chair and watched her and smoked one cigarette after another and listened to each and every sound she made. A number of times he had wanted to get up and go to her, to comfort her, but he did not move and he switched his eyes from her to the window and gradually it began to grow darker, with the pale autumn sun slipping behind a fold of chilly clouds. She had stopped crying long before.

— Are you all right? he asked.

— Yes.

— Why did you come today? I mean *today*, and not before?

— I've been ill.

— Ill, or drunk? His voice was not hard, it was a simple question.

— Drunk, she replied, whispering.

They were silent again for a long time.

— What pulled you together now, enough for you to come?

— I suppose Zach told you I came to see him?

— No, he didn't mention it. Why did you do that? And when?

— About two weeks ago. I woke up one morning and two and a half months had passed. She held out her hand and wiggled her fingers indicating she wanted a cigarette. He passed them to her across the table. I went to see, ah, Zach, as I said, and I got drunk. But I was already beginning to come out of it and I remember certain things that were said, that I said, and the most— important thing I remember is that I said I would go onto the stand at your trial and swear that you were sleeping with me—the whole time, that night.

— But why did you come *today?*

— I was told to come.

— Who told you to?

— Sheriff Cabell, she said quietly. He said that I was to convince you to see him, just to have a talk with him, and one word from him and you would go free.

— Did he say how he would accomplish that? Cornell asked, feeling the pressure for the first time since he had been arrested.

— No.

Cornell got up and walked quickly to the window. He did not have to think very hard or be very hypothetical to see what Cabell wanted and how with one word he could set Cornell free.

— He probably knows who the real murderer is, he said aloud, looking out of the window. And he wants The Recreation Hall in exchange.

— Is it that simple? she asked, incredulity in her voice.

— Probably, he said.

— Would he really let you—*die* to—to get The Recreation Hall?

— Yes, Cornell said. He would. And if you get rid of Cabell, which I could very easily do, then another one would take his place. It's all in the way things are. Tyrants have been slain before. Yet we still live with tyrants.

— Oh, God!

— I thought you would have learned at least that in New York, he said quietly. I did learn it, but I was lulled into thinking it didn't exist by the sophistry and the dishonest morality I found here in St. Johns Landing. Now I see that there is no way out and that we must all go down into a deep and sound sleep. Not disturbed by foolish dreams. A friend of mine said that once. Nick the Greek, the gambler. A wise man. A determined opponent of a true meaning in life. He was the only man I ever met that did not cop a plea, who did not wail and whine over what life had done to him.

He turned from the window and his view of the courtyard and the rude hickory trees and looked at her. It was not shocking to see that she was no longer attractive or female and that she was a shadowy drunk, what was shocking to him was that she had had so little faith in herself. Wasn't that the way it was everywhere, he thought. It did not make any difference where he was or when, Siam after the rains or Puerto Rico in January or New York in spring, the faces he remembered were all the same faces. Was all of life to be so painful that there wasn't time enough to discover your central position, your identity, and then live with it? Resignation and disgust for the way things had ended suddenly filled him with outrage and he pressed his eyes closed and balled his fists. It was all so goddamn absurd, and he opened his eyes, aware for the first time that he knew the value of nothing and the meaning of nothing and the whole of his life was a sum total of cruelty, despair, pain and indifference.

— Tell Cabell to go to see Zach. Tell Zach to do whatever is necessary to get me out of here. No questions. Give Cabell anything he wants or demands.

— I think, she said, I think he wants to sleep with me.

— But I don't think that will be part of the deal, he said coldly. Cabell is the classic middle-class European organizer, home-grown style. Petty mind, petty thinking, petty demands, petty conquests. The people who make the world go round. The organizers, the scared ones, the lice, who want it locked up.

— Is that what you think of me? A petty conquest? she asked.

— You're being sensitive and female.

— I'm a woman who has made many errors in her life and who is now trying to make up for them, she said desperately.

— And you are incapable of doing it yourself! he said vehemently.

— I need your help. You'll be free in three hours.

— To do what?

— Make a life with me, if you want it.

— And if I don't want it?

— I didn't mean to qualify it, she said. You will be free. With or without me.

— Free to do what! he demanded. To—to—

— Don't say any more, she said. Don't, don't—say—

She stood and started for the door. He remained standing at the window looking out.

— Goodbye, Harry. I don't know where I'm going, but if you want me enough, you'll find me.

He looked out of the window and did not respond. She pressed the buzzer.

37

The arrangements were simple enough. Zach handled the whole thing, but Carolyn was in sufficient control of herself not to meet Cabell alone again, and the whole thing was done in Zach's office in Winchester the next day. Terrible was brought into the negotiations and for ten per cent of the bar receipts he took title to The Recreation Hall; ten per cent of the entire gross, including the business from Mrs. Pitt's girls, would go into an account for Cornell's son. Cabell made a private deal with A. D. Benhide.

That night in The Recreation Hall, Cabell arrested Chigger for the murder of Delila Cornell. Chigger confessed before a stunned and unbelieving group of customers that included some drinkers from Washington who were seen to slip out of the garden door so that they would not be involved.

— I just wanted to tell her what a good man Harry

was, Chigger cried. He's everything a man should be, don't you see? He was good and kind and he had friends and he understood. Most of all he understood and that's what I tried to tell Delila—why, I knowed Delila ever since we went to the Cottage School together—Harry, why, Harry is something to be called on when you're way down. *He never once threw me out of his place!* She wouldn't listen to me, Chigger sobbed. I wanted to explain to her that I could straighten up, that I could and I would have! Let Harry go, let him have what he wanted, let me show her how I could be as good as Harry! She started to scream—

Chigger laid his head on the bar.

—I loved them both, he said between his sobs. I used to look at them walking on Sundays with the baby, she was so pretty and Harry was so—so—

He wept. Terrible tried to get him to take a drink. The pool-players stood like Vatican guards with their striped shirts and heavy boots and autumn hunting hats, their pool cues aligned with their bodies as if they were staves of defense. Colonel Sami had heard it all before, and he did not move and sat drinking and looking out of the front door as he had always done.

—I wouldn't of let Harry die. I just wanted him to think about what he had done, fuckin' around with that New York woman and all. Don't you see? That's what *I* wanted! Friends like Terrible, and a son, and a woman like Delila, and a place to come to like The Recreation Hall. He had it *all*, and he thrown it away on that New York woman!

Chigger spun off the bar, Cabell right after him, but Chigger went no further than Colonel Sami's table. He stood, weaving drunkenly with both hands on the table, upsetting the bottle of wine.

— Do you know what it costs to have a friend like you! he screamed at Colonel Sami. It's the cost of the whole world and everything in it. It—it makes the world go around. And all I got is disgusting people—

— Another bottle of wine, Terrible. And a glass for my friend.

— We ain't got time for that, Cabell said.

— *Achtung!* Colonel Sami said, rising, snapping to attention and staring Cabell in the eye, staring him down. *You will do as I say!*

Cabell stopped cold and looked at the Colonel. He remembered the sheriff of Winchester County and the college boy and he obliged.

— I am your friend, Chigger, Colonel Sami said. Chigger had his head on the table and his thin body shook with sobs. Colonel Sami reached out and touched Chigger's shoulder and comforted him. I am your friend, Chigger. It is not what a man does, he said quietly, but what his motives are. That is our life, yours and mine.

— *But I loved them both!* Chigger said, hoarsely.

— We both loved them, Chigger, you and I. People like us always love those who are sure and unafraid and do not realize what they have. And they are such important people, Chigger, and we are so unimportant, that we can't help loving them.

209

38

At first snow, with the orchards bare and the first freeze turning the snow into ice, St. Johns Landing was camping around open fires after a day of working frozen snow off the delicate apple branches. The murder of Delila and the affair of Harry Cornell and Carolyn had ceased to be the main topic of conversation. Chigger had been convicted of second-degree murder, that is, there was no premeditation and it was generally accepted that Chigger was too drunk to know that he had raped Delila. He was doing twenty years to life.

No one knew where Carolyn had gone, but they all knew that Harry Cornell had gone to Baltimore for a ship. There was talk, but no proof, that Colonel Sami, Mrs. DuPays and Terrible had received a card from him from somewhere in Europe. But this was not true. No one had heard from him at all. None of the regulars came to The Recreation Hall any more. Mrs. Pitt's girls had ruined that. The record player had been replaced by a jukebox. The good people of St. Johns Landing did not know that they missed what had been before.

— It's just not the same as it was, they said around their kerosene campfires. Something, something had gone out of their lives which they missed, and they could not say what it was.

39

Harry Cornell stood on the bridge of his ship taking the four-to-eight watch in the middle of a dead sea that is due south of Ceylon in the Indian Ocean. He stood his watch and searched the skies and the never-changing deadline of the horizon. He watched falling stars, the rising of the moon, the Love Star and the Southern Cross and listened to the rock'n'roll of the young crew having a party in the crew mess.

They had smuggled a woman aboard for the crossing. It was all very funny and good and everybody was racking up experience they could talk about in the bars on Tenth Avenue, East Ham, Singapore. But he was not with it. He was the old man on the bridge who left his watch and went to the saloon, ate, and then went to his room and got drunk. A new group, another bunch, another sentimentality rearing up and demanding atten- tion. But for Harry Cornell, it was over. He had never been able to understand what love was. He only now understood that love was the only way.

He stood alone on the wing of the bridge in the middle of a dirty hot ocean and it came upon him. He cried for Delila, but it was too late; he cried for Carolyn, but it was too late; he cried for Chigger, Colonel Sami, Terrible, Josephine DuPays—but it was too late. He was crying over what might have been.

The man on the wheel saw and heard the mate crying. He felt himself stir. Tears came to his eyes. For a moment, in his own private hell, he too cried for what might have been.